I dedicate this book to the love of my life, Michael. You have been my heart for fifty wonderful years.

Acknowledgements

It has taken quite a few people to bring this book to see the light of day. I'm especially grateful to the following people for all of their help.

Jan Pippins, Lori Roberts Herbst, Sue Carrigan, Sharon Jensen, June Kosier for being my Beta readers.

I am especially grateful for the invaluable help from my two critique groups:

The GFWG—Zach Richards, Billy Neary, AJ Davidson, Kay Hafner, Robin Inwald, Sandy Buxton, Bill Thomas

The Storyboarders—Roxyanne Young, Lisa Rondinelli Alberts, Candie Moonshower

Mega thanks go to my publisher—Gemma Halliday for believing in Sam and Porkchop and Susie Halliday for her terrific editing. Thank you both so much for making my dream come true.

CHAPTER ONE

———

Who would have guessed this would be a good day for a murder? When I left home this morning the sky was a robin's egg blue streaked with wispy clouds. The digital thermometer in my ten-year-old, egg-yolk yellow Volkswagen Bug read sixty-eight. The local weather person on my car's radio predicted a sunny day, with the temperature climbing into the nineties by late afternoon. Not typical weather for Upstate New York. Eighties were usually the highest we experienced during the summer, but I will take it over the frigid cold of winter. Nope, murder didn't hover on the horizon. Hot weather yes, murder, no.

"Porkchop, come on. Get those chubby legs moving. We have a lot to do this morning." My beloved dachshund stretched his long red body on the passenger seat of my convertible. He cocked his head and shot me a look as if to say "How dare you impugn my svelte physique? I am the star of your soon-to-be-hit seller—*Porkchop, The Wonder Dog*."

Parked in front of my favorite hangout, The Ewe and Me Woolery, I turned off the car's ignition. We hookers fondly called it The Ewe. Now don't go raising your eyebrows so high they flip into your cranium. I'm a hooker—a rug hooker that is. Besides enjoying rug hooking, I am also a children's writer, mostly freelance magazine writing, but right now—fingers, toes, and eyes crossed—my picture book starring Porkchop, sat in the final stages of approval on the editor's desk at Rolling Brook Press.

I got out of my car and walked around to the passenger door. Porkchop looked up at me through the open window with his liquid brown eyes. "Sugar plum, I know I am disturbing your beauty sleep, but we have a bunch of errands to run this morning." I reached in and snagged him off the car seat. I clipped on his leash then set him on the sidewalk next to me.

The Ewe and Me Woolery stood proudly in a turn-of-the-century brick storefront on Glen Street in Wings Falls, my hometown in Upstate New York. I knew I had arrived early. The Bug's clock only read eight thirty and the doors weren't open for business for another hour. In my mind's eye, I could imagine Lucy Foster, who along with her husband Ralph, owned The Ewe, bustling around the shop, straightening shelves, and rearranging patterns for us woolaholics. We couldn't get enough of the fabulous wool and goodies her shop offered.

Morning sunlight streamed in from the windows and shone on the cubbies lining the walls of her shop. They were stuffed with wool ranging in color from bright pinks, greens, blues, and every color of the rainbow, to the more primitive, or as Lucy liked to call them "muddy" tans, creams, and muted hues of the spectrum, the colors I gravitated to myself. If you needed a specific color, Lucy had it or would conjure it up in her marvelous dye kitchen in the back of the store.

The Ewe held a special place in my heart. My Loopy Ladies, fellow hookers who gathered at the shop, saw me through a rough patch five years ago. My then-husband of twenty-five years, George, announced he wanted a divorce. We own a funeral parlor together, The Do Drop Inn Funeral Parlor. I know, a crazy name for a funeral home, but for years a bar occupied the building before we purchased it and the locals preferred the name to Davies Funeral Parlor.

Being young and newly married I'd wanted to help the hubby with his career, so I'd used an inheritance left to me from an uncle to purchase it. Silly me. Apparently, George forgot what I'd done all those years ago to help fulfill his dream of having his own funeral parlor. And—also apparently—his late-night corpse pickups had involved more live bodies than dead. At least one unquestionably live body, our secretary, Anna. He'd had the nerve to puff out his chest with pride and tell me while I made him breakfast one morning, "Samantha, Anna and I are expecting."

With a confused look on my face, I'd turned from the stove and asked, "Expecting, what?"

He'd had the decency to fidget in his chair. "Twins."

My eyes widened. "As in babies?"

He'd blushed and nodded.

It still does my heart good to think of how I had dumped a plate of pancakes smothered in warm maple syrup on his neatly pressed khaki-clad lap. What smarted the most? We'd tried for years to conceive a child of our own. We'd traveled from one specialist to another seeking help with our problem. Final diagnosis, George's low sperm count. But, one of those little buggers had hit its mark, though, resulting in Harry and Larry.

My Southern Belle cousin and best friend, Candie Parker's, opinion about summed up mine when she'd said, "Good riddance to an ol' trash sucking possum." Candie worked as a part-time secretary for our town's mayor, Mark Hogan. She also wrote romance novels under the pen name Candie del'Amore. I thought of her as an expert in the romance department, having been engaged eleven times. Her novels had a large following, but she knew the reading public was too fickle for her to give up her day job. I think she secretly had a crush on Mark, though. They kept everything professional at the office, but I know they'd had a few dates. This time I rooted for Mark. He was a keeper.

A light shone in the back of The Ewe. I knocked on the door and peered through the glass. Sure enough, Lucy scurried from the back of the store, a coffee mug clutched in her hand.

She swung the door open to let Porkchop and me in. "Why, Samantha Davies, what brings you here so early. My goodness, it's Saturday morning. Don't you sleep in?"

A retired Home Economics teacher in her late sixties, Lucy bent and scratched between my dachshund's ears. "How's my favorite shop dog?" Porkchop closed his eyes and leaned into her hand. His tail wagged in warp speed as he basked in her attention.

"Lucy, you've spoiled him to the point he's impossible to live with after spending time here." True, my dog often accompanied me when I came to The Ewe, especially during our Monday morning "hook-ins" when the Loopy Ladies gathered to hook, eat, and dish the local gossip. Our group ranged in age from our youngest thirtysomething, Susan Mayfield, who with her husband Brian, co-owned Momma Mia's, and in my opinion the best Italian restaurant this side of

NYC. To Gladys O'Malley, who would never admit to her eighty-two years. Gladys also lived next door to me and thought it her life's mission to find me a "beau" as she called her many attempts to set me up with a date. So far, I'd managed to dodge her well-meaning efforts to end my single lifestyle.

Lucy's rounded figure shook as she laughed. Shoulder-length white hair bounced about the collar of her blouse as she lifted Porkchop's chin. "But look at those sweet eyes. Who wouldn't fall in love with them?" He closed his eyes and let out a sigh. I swear he knew when people heaped compliments on him, which he deemed were well deserved.

"I'm sorry to disturb you so early, but I need another piece of the smoky blue wool you dyed so I can finish the sky in my ocean-scape rug."

"Yes, yes, I have some more back in the dye room. Follow me and I'll fetch it for you."

My eyes bounced around the familiar sights of the store as Porkchop, and I trailed behind her. Besides the cubbies lining the wood-clad walls, wool flowed out of an antique pie safe and from ornate Victorian dresser drawers. My fingers itched to pick through a vintage dry sink. It bulged with Lucy's hand-drawn rug hooking patterns. Like every other hooker, I already anticipated the next rug I wanted on my frame.

Nestled in a room off her main studio sat the dye room or what we called the "zone of magic." A stove and sink lined one wall, separated by a multi-colored dye-stained Formica countertop, attesting to the many times Lucy brewed up fabulous colors in giant white enamel pots. Occasionally, she invited me and her followers to join in and create a pot or two of color.

A raised wooden oak table stood in the middle of the room. Attached to one end sat strippers. I guess we hookers can't get away from the whole sexual connotation thing. These hand-cranked machines contained a disk with blades for cutting our material into narrow pieces of wool for our hooked masterpieces. The wool strips varied in width from narrow, about an eighth of an inch for the fine hookers who want to obtain a more realistic-looking design in their rugs, to my preference, quarter of an inch or wider strips for a more primitive-looking rug. But Lucy also used this table to draw out the rug patterns I and the other Loopy Ladies dearly loved to hook.

"Now where did I put your wool?" Lucy scratched the top of her head and sent her glasses flying. "Drat." She bent to pick them off the floor. "Oh my, here it is." She laughed and pulled the smoky blue wool from a basket tucked under the worktable. "Sometimes, I wonder if I'd remember my name if I didn't have it printed on my driver license."

I joined in her laughter. "Thanks, Lucy. You are a lifesaver. What do I owe you?" I reached into my designer handbag, a weakness of mine. I couldn't get enough of them. I would search eBay for the best price on a "gently" used one I could fit into my limited budget. Oh, well at least it's a legal addiction. From today's handbag of choice, a brown and black striped Fendi, I drew out my wallet and plucked a couple of bills from its usually dusty interior.

She waved a hand at me. "Never mind. Pay me Monday morning when we meet. I don't have my cash drawer open, yet."

Since I lived only two blocks from The Ewe, in the same brick ranch house where I'd grown up, she knew where to find me. Often, when I needed a break from writing, Porkchop and I stopped in The Ewe for a hooking fix. After my divorce from George, my parents had signed the house over to me and moved to sunny Florida. They claimed they'd had enough of shoveling snow. Frankly, I think they wanted the party lifestyle their friends, Marge and Herb Feinstein, enjoyed in their retirement village.

Lucy leaned against a scarred pine desk. It served as her check-out counter and asked, "Besides needing wool, what brings you and my friend"—she nodded at Porkchop—"out so early this lovely morning?"

I looked at my better half, curled at my feet. "He, I fear, has developed into a food snob. The other day I'd bought a bag of a new gourmet dog food, Burger Bites. The one advertised on television every other commercial break. I thought he'd love it. Fido on TV gobbles a bowlful and lets out a happy howl. But my buddy here turned his nose up and strutted out of the room when I filled his bowl. He loves his Mighty Nuggets, period. I guess he doesn't like his food horizons expanded. I thought Calvin Perkins could use the Burger Bites at the shelter." Calvin owned For Pet's Sake, the local pet shelter.

People, he didn't like so much. I'd heard some grumble that they never even got a "thank you" out of him when they made a donation to the shelter. Manners was not his middle name. But he loved animals, from snakes to ferrets and everything in between. The shelter always needed donations, so Porkchop's loss would become the shelter's gain.

Lucy crossed her arms and tapped her foot. "Humph, Calvin Perkins. That old sourpuss. How he manages to keep his shelter open, I don't know. The other day at the Shop and Save, I wanted to purchase a couple steaks for Ralph's dinner. Anyway, I saw a couple of really nice ones that would be perfect for the barbeque when a hand reached in front of me and grabbed them right out from under my nose. I turned to see who was acting so rude and it was—Calvin Perkins. He even bumped his shopping cart into me, so I'd move out of his way. And did he apologize—nope. Ralph sure wasn't happy when I told him about what had happened. He was ready to march over to the shelter and give Calvin a piece of his mind. It took a little talking to sooth Ralph's feathers down. Frankly, I don't think Calvin knows the meaning of the word polite. Being so nasty, he must have won the lottery because I don't know who would give him money for his shelter.

"You're right, he can be cantankerous." I peeked at my watch, a worn Timex my parents had given me when I graduated from high school. To paraphrase the old ad, "it had taken a licking and kept on ticking." Unlike my handbags, I had no desire for a designer watch. "I better get going. Calvin doesn't trust anyone but himself to check in donations. He told me to arrive before nine if I wanted to drop it off." I shook my head. Did he think any of the volunteers at the shelter wanted to steal the dog food? Maybe kibble thieves ran rampant in Wings Falls. "Besides, I have an article deadline." I needed to hit the send button on my computer today or lose my advance on an article about the life cycle of the hummingbird moth for *Kid Science Magazine.* Not the most thrilling subject, but a paying gig is a paying gig. I'd already spent the money on a gently used Coach handbag I'd found on eBay.

The bell over The Ewe's wooden front door jingled when I pulled it open to leave. I gave Lucy a final wave then tugged gently on Porkchop's leash to signal it was time to hit the road.

"Sammie!"

I sighed deeply and groaned. I was only a few feet from my car. Gladys O'Malley, her orange hair permed tighter than a Brillo pad, bobbled towards me. My guess, since this was the middle of August and September was only a few weeks away, the orange color signaled the coming of autumn. Gladys dyed her hair to celebrate holidays, the change of seasons or anything tickling her fancy.

"Yes," I said and peeked at my watch. I didn't want to act rude. She was a widow after all, but she could easily talk my ear off for a good hour. Her dearly departed husband, Captain Stan, had sailed the seas as a fisherman. His flaking wooden, thirty-foot boat now sailed the seas of crabgrass and unmowed lawn in her backyard. An urn containing his ashes sat behind the ship's wheel.

Gladys came to a halt in front of my dog and me. "I've invited my nephew, Junior, for dinner next Saturday night. He's new in town. Can you join us?"

"Gee, I will have to check my calendar." What was with people? Being single didn't curse me. In fact, the last five years had treated me well. Maybe I'm a little lonely at times, but I had no one to answer to. Well, except Porkchop, of course.

"Okay, let me know. I will see you Monday." Gladys waved, her scrawny upper arm waggled back and forth as she walked towards The Ewe. Lucy stood in the store's front door and turned over the open sign.

To attract my dog's attention, I patted my jeans-clad leg. Jeans, yoga pants, and T-shirts were my preferred attire. "Come on boy, time to hit the road and do our good deed for the day." Little did I know I would soon become the poster child for the old saying "No good deed goes unpunished."

CHAPTER TWO

———

I nosed the Bug out of the parking space. If the traffic light gods blessed me with only green lights, I would arrive at For Pet's Sake in plenty of time.

Ten minutes later, I pulled into the shelter's front parking lot. I peeked at the Bug's clock and heaved a sigh of relief, eight-fifty. I turned to Porkchop, who lay curled next to me on the passenger seat. "We made it. And on time." My dog opened one eye then closed it. "I hate to disturb your beauty sleep again, but I don't want to make Calvin any grouchier than he already is by being late."

The sound of car tires squealing on the back parking lot of the building drew my attention. Porkchop's head rose off the seat and a low growl rumbled up from his throat. "Sounds as if someone has left in a hurry. Calvin must be here. I see his pickup, and the side door of the shelter looks ajar. Do you think he propped it open for me?" This puzzled me since Calvin couldn't count chivalry as one of his better traits. His battered brown pickup truck with the rear bumper wired on sat parked next to the door.

I leaned over the back seat of my car and heaved the bag of dog food up next to Porkchop. I snatched his leash out of the pocket in my door and clipped it onto his collar. "Come on boy, we've got a lot to do today." I stepped out of the car and hefted the Burger Bites onto my shoulder. My pup hopped out of the car and trotted in front of me into the shelter.

"Calvin, it's Sam, Samantha Davies. I've brought the Burger Bites," I called out while I nudged the metal door farther open with my foot. I gripped Porkchop's leash and shoved the bulky bag of dog food up my shoulder. With a yip, he jerked forward. His leash tore out of my hand, and he raced down the hall with the leash trailing after him, slapping against the tile floor.

"Porkchop, Porkchop, stop. Come back." I chased after him, calling his name. The bag of dog food bounced on my shoulder. The one thing my dog had mastered from all his years of obedience classes—how not to follow my orders. When he was on a mission, he listened to no one, but himself.

As I ran down the cinder block hallway, a strong scent filled my nose. Not the usual smell of the disinfectant used for cleaning up animal poop and urine I associated with the shelter. No, the odor tickling my nose as I ran after my dog was sweet and spicy, a combination of cinnamon mixed with a rosy aroma, more like a perfume. Oh, well maybe Calvin's cleaning staff scrubbed the place with a new cleanser.

I rounded the corner to the reception area and skidded to a stop. Porkchop lay on the tile floor, chewing on a bone longer than his body and almost as wide around. I'd seen bones like the one Porkchop was now in love with at our local butcher shop, Meat Of The Matter. The owner, Angelo Condi, let nothing go to waste there. Not even the bones from the animals he rendered into steaks and chops. But this was the biggest one I'd ever seen. It must have come from one huge bovine. "What do you have there?" I lowered the Burger Bites to the floor and slowly approached my wayward dog. I may be his mom, but he would defend his new bone with his life if I tried to take it from him. I valued my fingers too much.

"Oops! What the…?" I gasped as I slipped on the floor. I looked down and noticed small nuggets of dog food littering the floor.

Then I saw them. Sneaker-clad feet poked out from behind the reception desk. I ran the short distance to the desk. Someone lay on the floor, partially covered in large bags of kibble. My hands trembled as I tugged at the heavy bags of dog food, trying to uncover the person. Several of the bags split open, and their contents spilled out onto the floor. Because the bags weighed at least forty pounds each this became no easy task. From the shape of the person's legs, I could tell it was a man lying beneath the bags of kibble, but I couldn't make out his identity. Not for sure, although I had an idea who it might be. I pushed and tugged while Porkchop squatted and enjoyed the bone.

At last, I uncovered the body. My shaking hands flew to my mouth, my suspicions confirmed. "Oh, no." The short, squat body sprawled on the floor was Calvin Perkins. I placed a finger on his leathery neck and checked for a pulse, but found none. Nothing, not even a blip. Blood pooled on the floor next to his head and matted the little hair covering it. He lay on the floor looking very dead. I stood and backed away from him. I don't know why my body shook so much. It's not like I hadn't been in contact with my share of dead bodies at the funeral parlor, but this was different, I had never discovered those bodies. They were part of the business. They arrived already dead when they got to The Do Drop. My ex George dealt with them. My job was to take care of the business's paperwork.

I reached into my purse and fumbled around for my cell phone. I flipped it open and yes, I still use a flip phone. My legs shook so badly I needed to sink onto the faux leather rolling chair behind the reception counter before I flopped on the floor next to Calvin.

Light-headedness washed over me. I lowered my head between my knees for a moment, then dialed 9-1-1. With the blood rushing to my head, I quickly told the operator about the body sprawled at my feet. She asked how I knew the person was dead. I replied my biggest hint was the blood oozing on the floor near his head plus his lack of breathing. I gave her my location. She said the police and EMTs would arrive shortly and to stay put until they arrived. The operator added she would remain on the line until they got here, but I told her it was not necessary and hung up.

Porkchop abandoned the bone and trotted over to Calvin. He sniffed Calvin then licked his hand. I guess he thought he should lick the hand that had gifted him with a bone longer than his sausage-shaped body and almost as round. It took me a few seconds for my brain to register his actions before I tugged on his collar to pull him away from Calvin. I didn't think the police would appreciate a hand covered in dachshund spit. He returned to gnawing on the bone, but he left a trail of bloody footprints in his wake.

"Look at the mess you made." I tied his leash to a corner of the reception room's scarred wooden desk so he couldn't wander over to Calvin again then looked around the room for paper towels and cleanser to clean up the footprints. I found what I needed for the task in a dented metal cabinet in a corner of the room across from the reception desk. I sprayed the floor and knelt to wipe up the prints. The strong ammonia smell didn't help my roiling stomach. I have a big aversion to the sight of blood of any kind, especially my own.

"Ma'am, leave the spray bottle on the floor, stand up slowly, raise your hands. Back away from the body," commanded a deep male voice behind me.

I groaned. I would know this voice until the day I died. My nemesis, Joe Peters. I hadn't heard him enter the shelter. Like me, he must have used the side door. He has hated me since preschool when I told the teacher he had peed in the playground sandbox. I didn't consider myself a goodie-two-shoes, but who wanted to play in sand he had used as his toilet? It was not my fault the school janitor had to dump out the sandbox and we couldn't play in it for a week while he sterilized the box. And I also don't consider it my fault that kids have a long memory and have called him Sandy throughout school and afterwards.

I stood and slowly turned. With my hands raised, I waggled my fingers at him. "Hi, Joe." He returned my greeting with a scowl on his pudgy face.

Porkchop looked up from the bone and growled.

"It's okay, boy. It's only Sergeant Peters." I flashed Joe a weak smile. "Can I put my arms down now?"

He groaned even louder, but lowered the gun he'd aimed at me. "What are you doing here?" he spat out between gritted teeth. His unibrow furrowed in disgust. I imagine he was as unhappy at finding me at the scene of an accident as I was at being here. I hadn't run into Joe in a while, not having any reason to call the local law enforcement, but I sure hoped the thirty-seven years since graduating high school together had treated me better than him. The buttons of his gray uniform shirt strained against the paunch of his belly. He holstered his gun then removed his cap and swiped a hand over his receding hairline. What little hair remained on his head had turned silver. I made a mental note to hit the gym ASAP and check in with my hairstylist so only she would know if any gray had crept into my mane.

I was not about to let him intimidate me. "Well, Sandy, oops I mean Joe." If it was possible, his unibrow furrowed even more. He ground his teeth together. "Porkchop didn't care for a bag of dog food I had bought him, so I wanted to donate it to Calvin's shelter. You know, instead of it going to waste."

Joe shook his head in disbelief. "Humph. I never heard of a dog turning its nose up at perfectly good food before. How do I know you didn't kill Calvin? Did he get fresh with you and you whacked him? "

Now Joe was getting my dander up. I placed my hands on my hips and jutted out my chin. "No, I didn't kill him. He was already dead when we arrived. My Porkchop is a discriminating eater. As I already told you, I didn't want the dog food to go to waste." I wanted to poke the man in the chest with my finger to emphasize my point but was afraid he would arrest me for assaulting a police officer. Was I going to find myself behind bars because of a kindergarten grudge? I shook my head to clear it of such silly thoughts. Calvin's death had to be accidental.

"How did you get into the shelter? Calvin doesn't usually open up until ten."

"I arranged with Calvin to meet him here at nine. I arrived a few minutes before nine and found the door on the side of the building propped open. I figured since he knew I was coming he'd opened it up for me. As I entered the building Porkchop pulled out of my hand. When I caught up with my dog, I found him and Calvin in the reception area." Porkchop in bone heaven and Calvin, hopefully, in celestial heaven.

"Were you aware of anyone else in the shelter when you arrived? Volunteers?" Joe asked.

Brown curls bounced about my shoulders as I shook my head. "No."

From the frown on his face, I could tell he was having a hard time believing me. I knew he'd love to lock me up and throw away the key.

Sirens blared outside the shelter's cinder block walls. A man who had come in with Joe walked over to the scarred wooden front doors and unlocked them. Two EMTs in navy jumpsuits with stethoscopes hanging around their necks burst into the room.

The man, who I guessed was another officer, directed them to the "body," as Calvin was now known. He conferred with the EMTs in a hushed tone. The EMTs pointed to the side of Calvin's head. The officer scribbled in a small notebook he had fished from the inner pocket of his tweed sports jacket then he tucked it back into his coat pocket and pulled out a cell phone. He punched in some numbers and turned his back on Joe and me so he could talk privately, I assumed.

I nodded towards the supposed officer and asked Joe, "Who's that?"

"Detective Hank Johnson. He's with our CID unit, Criminal Investigative Department. He's new on the force, transferred here from Albany. He's riding along with me so I can familiarize him with the area."

Detective Johnson pulled away from the EMTs and walked over to Joe and me. I couldn't help but notice how handsome he was. Dark, wavy brown hair with a lock falling over his forehead. My fingers itched to smooth it back. At least six feet with piercing blue eyes set in an olive-toned face. He made George Clooney look like chump change.

"Joe, I called Judge Thompson for a search warrant." Then with a slight nod of his head he said, "Ma'am."

I shook my head to bring me back to the present. I felt like a real dolt. Geez, he had to be at least ten years younger than me. What was I thinking? And with poor Calvin splayed out on the floor across the room.

I smoothed errant curls behind my ears. "Yes, Detective Johnson."

He raised an eyebrow at me, surprised I'm sure, I knew his name.

"She was curious as to who you were, Hank, so I filled her in." I wanted to stomp on Joe's highly polished shoes but, again, didn't want to get arrested for assaulting a policeman. Don't get me wrong I have the highest regard for our men and women of law enforcement, but with our history, Joe and I get along as well as mixing oil and water. Joe had made it sound like I lusted after the detective. Guess this was payback time for my big mouth in kindergarten. Talk about holding a grudge. I could have melted into my cowboy boots.

"You are the one who found the victim?" Detective Johnson pulled his note book out of his coat pocket again and flipped it open.

"Victim? Wasn't this an accident?" My voice quivered. I thought Calvin had met with an accident. I figured he'd slipped and fallen, hit his head on the floor, and it caused the stack of kibbles to topple on him.

"Can't tell for sure, yet. I will leave it to the medical examiner to determine. I'm not ruling anything out. What brought you here?"

I didn't like the tone of his voice. My back stiffened. His gruff voice sounded as if I had a motive to do Calvin in. So much for my first impression of him as handsome and charming. I stared into his not so beautiful blue eyes and again, as I had done moments before to Joe, relayed my reason for coming to the shelter and how Porkchop escaped my hold and discovered Calvin behind the reception desk. See if I'll ever be altruistic again if I am rewarded with a grilling by a detective new to the area. Did he bring any brass knuckles with him from Albany? Or did he have a Billy Club stashed under the front seat of his patrol car?

"Porkchop?" A smile curved the detective's lips.

"Yes, anything wrong with his name?" Detective Johnson, questioning my choice of name for my dog, did not endear him to me, either.

He grinned. "When I was a kid, I had watched the same *Doug Funnie* cartoons."

What an inane conversation to have with poor Calvin soon to leave the shelter in a body bag, but I smiled despite the situation. "Yes, I loved those cartoons, too."

Detective Johnson snapped his notebook shut and tucked it back into his jacket pocket. "I need you to come to the Wings Falls Police Station to make an official statement."

"Can I drop my dog off at home first?" Porkchop lay on the floor, still gnawing on the bone in front of the desk.

Detective Johnson nodded and turned to him. "What's this?" He pointed at the bone.

The detective reached down with his rubber-gloved hand and tried to extract the bone from Porkchop. He growled, my dog I mean, but at this point, I wouldn't be surprised if

Detective Johnson growled, too. Porkchop clamped his jaws down on the bone, not about to give it up without a fight.

"Ms. Davies can you get your dog to relinquish the bone. See that red stain." He pointed to the unchewed end of the bone. "It looks like it may have blood on it. It could possibly be Calvin's. Your dog might be destroying key evidence."

I gulped. "As in murder?"

He nodded his head. "Yes, as in murder."

Maybe my earlier thoughts weren't so silly after all, and Joe would make me a murder suspect.

CHAPTER THREE

———

I bribed Porkchop with a handful of the kibble scattered on the reception area floor to get him to relinquish the "evidence" bone. Then, like I'd told the detective, I took him home but became delayed by Gladys. When I pulled into my driveway, she leapt up from her wicker rocker and raced down the porch steps as fast as her bird legs would move.

"Sam, Sam." She waved a lace handkerchief to get my attention. She reminded me of a character in one of those old cruise ship posters waving bon voyage to the poor people on shore who couldn't afford to sail on the Queen Elizabeth II. Out of breath, she halted by my car door. She grabbed onto the handle and leaned in my open window. The scent of her lilac perfume filled my car. My nose twitched as I put my hand over it and tried to stifle the sneeze that wanted to escape. Porkchop wasn't as lucky. Three large sneezes shook his body. "Do you know what happened at the shelter? My scanner reported an incident there. They called for an ambulance. I'm so worried about my Frank."

Gladys listened to her police scanner day and night. Way into the early morning hours, I can hear it screeching if my bedroom windows were cracked open. Hard of hearing, Gladys, cranks it up to full volume. Half of the neighborhood must hear what's happening, too. No one complains though, since this is her chief form of entertainment, other than trying to fix me up with a date.

I frowned. How did she know I'd stopped there? Did she have a crystal ball?

Gladys must have read the confused look on my face. Her fingers twisted the handkerchief she had waved a minute ago. "Lucy mentioned where you went after you left The Ewe. Remember dear, I saw you outside The Ewe this morning? I figured I would stop in and chat with her after you passed me coming out of her store. So, I knew where you were headed. Did you see my Frank? He said he wanted to give old sourpuss Calvin some money. I tell Frank it's enough that he volunteers his time there helping to take care of those sweet animals. I don't know why he even associates with such a cranky old man, but I don't butt into Frank's business. I'm not a nosy person. But you know Frank, he loves animals and even Calvin's crabby temper won't keep him from tending those poor abandoned creatures." She tucked the mangled handkerchief into the bodice of the cotton house dress covering her scrawny bosom.

I coughed—more like sputtered. Lake George would freeze over in July before Gladys stopped poking her nose in everyone's business. And was it only this morning I had stumbled upon poor Calvin's body at For Pet's Sake?

Frank was also known as Frank Gilbert, or Gladys's "beau" as she liked to call him. He'd never take the captain's place, but she said he provided good company. He kept her toes warm on a cold winter's night. That tidbit I considered TMI. He worked a couple of nights a week at the Wings Falls Animal Hospital, cleaning the cages, feeding the dogs and cats in residence, making sure all remained well during the night shift. He had a magic touch with animals. When he wasn't at the animal hospital he usually volunteered at the shelter.

"No, I didn't notice him at the shelter. I'm sure he's fine." But then I remembered the sound of a car screeching out of the parking lot when I had arrived there. Could it have been Frank Gilbert? Why would he zoom out of the shelter's parking lot?

I told Gladys I needed to hurry and put Porkchop in the house before I went out again.

She pulled an iPhone out of the pocket of her housedress. Geez, even a woman in her eighties could handle a more technologically advanced phone than me. Gladys muttered to herself while she swiped her knobby fingers over its surface. I presumed she was dialing Frank's number. By the irritation in her voice as she stomped up the wooden steps, poor Frank better have a good excuse for his whereabouts and why he failed to answer his phone.

* * *

My hands trembled as I placed them on the steering wheel of my Bug and sat in the parking lot of the Wings Falls Police Station. I took a deep breath then said to myself, "Okay, I survived my meeting. Geez, how many ways could Detective Johnson ask the same question? Yes, I was there to donate a bag of kibble to the shelter. No, I hadn't noticed anyone else in the shelter when I arrived. And the kicker—did I have any personal dealings with Calvin Perkins? Was he implying that Calvin and I were having an affair? Oh, please. Even the thought of such a thing made my stomach queasy." I shut my mouth and looked around the parking lot. Besides me, I saw three black and white police cars parked out front of the station. I hope no one noticed while I ranted to myself. They'd think I was loony.

* * *

I stopped at the Wings Falls Animal Hospital after my meeting with Detective Johnson. After I'd repeated to him, for a second time, exactly what I had told Joe Peters earlier in the morning, he had my statement typed up and I signed it. I hoped it was the last time I would have to deal with Calvin's death. Although, it wasn't a great hardship talking to the handsome Detective Johnson, despite some of his questions getting under my skin.

Even though I still felt traumatized by finding Calvin's body this morning, Porkchop still needed more Mighty Nuggets and I preferred to buy them at the vet's rather than ordering them online. I also had an appointment with Doc Sorensen, the owner of the animal hospital. I wanted to interview him on his career as a veterinarian for an article I had proposed to a magazine.

"Sam, everything all right?" Jeanine Wagner's voice penetrated my thoughts and snapped me back to the present. Jeanine held down the hospital's reception area for Doc Sorenson, always with a friendly smile and a treat for the furry patients. She sat at a desk behind the reception counter staring at me. With good reason, too, because I'm sure I must have looked like a zombie with a blank look on my face. I still found it hard to grasp that my Porkchop and I had discovered Calvin Perkins' dead body only a few hours before.

"Yes, yes, I'm fine. I've had a horrible morning and afternoon. I sat in the police station for at least two hours and gave the new detective my statement. I think he thought if he asked me enough times about what I saw and why I went to the shelter I would change my story." Hank Johnson, if nothing else, was persistent. He'd learn soon enough Wings Falls wasn't Albany and those big city ways didn't go down well here. Folks in Wings Falls acted more laid back and considerate of each other. Oh, yes, he had much to learn, but I wasn't the one going to teach him.

Jeanine rose from her seat and walked over to the counter. It separated her from the rest of the waiting room. "Are you talking about Hank Johnson and Calvin Perkins?" she asked.

I guess the puzzled look on my face prompted her to add. "Oh, he's a new client. He has the most adorable bulldog named Nina."

My frown deepened. "How did you know about Calvin?"

"Gladys O'Malley. She phoned here looking for Frank and mentioned what happened at the shelter." Jeanine straightened a pile of pamphlets on neutering your pet sitting on the counter next to the treat jar.

Jeanine and I had attended high school together. She'd belonged to the popular crowd, the perky cheerleader who dated the captain of our school's football team, while I hung out with the bookworm group. After graduation, she went to High Peaks Community College while I shuffled off to Cornell.

When I'd come home for Thanksgiving freshman year, I'd run into her at Walmart. I would have walked right past her if we hadn't bumped into each other in the aspirin aisle. I gave her a cheery "hi." With her head bent, she mumbled a hello back. Gone was the always present smile, replaced by a pale, drawn complexion. She had pulled her dull brown hair into a slick ponytail. An over-sized sweater hung about her skeletal thin body. I'd asked her about Jacob, her high school boyfriend. Her head had jerked up and tears filled her eyes. She'd left her shopping cart in the middle of the aisle and scurried away. Later, when I told my mother about the encounter, she said

Jeanine and Jacob Sorenson had broken up and she'd dropped out of college the month before.

Since then, Jeanine had worked for Doc Sorenson at the Wings Falls Animal Hospital. Jacob was Doc's younger brother, but I guess it didn't bother Jeanine since Jacob settled in Las Vegas after graduating from college and rarely returned home. She knew everyone's pet by name and kept all their files up to date. You could say she ran the office for Doc. Without her, I don't think the place could function.

Jeanine shook her head and returned to her desk. "How awful. I wouldn't consider Calvin the most loved character in town, but I wouldn't wish him dead. Doc always donates any broken bags of pet food to the shelter. And if any of the animals have a medical problem, Doc never charges him for his services." She picked up a folder off her desk and stuffed a stack of papers into it.

"Wow, I didn't know that. It was certainly generous of Doc."

Jeanine nodded. "Yes, it was, but did Calvin appreciate Doc's kindness? No. Doc never got a thank you. Not once. Calvin acted as if it was all owed to him."

"I keep hearing he wasn't the nicest person in town," I said. "Oh, by the way I need a bag of Kibble for Porkchop."

Jeanine got up from her desk and walked over to the counter. "Sure, what size would you like? The twenty-pound or the forty-pound bag?"

"I know my pup is a small guy, but I find it more convenient buying the larger size plus it is more economical."

Jeanine nodded. "It certainly is. For the price of the bigger bag, it's like getting a small one free. With what you save you can buy more treats for Porkchop. I'll be right back with his Kibbles."

I laughed. "Doesn't he wish."

Jeanine returned in minutes cradling the large bag in her arms. "Here you go." She hefted the bag onto the counter.

I stared in amazement, remembering how heavy the bag of Mighty Nuggets was that I'd wanted to donate to the shelter. "Geez, you sling that bag around like it was a sack of feathers."

Jeanine flexed her muscles and laughed. "I get a pretty good workout hauling these bags up front from the storeroom."

"I guess you do. It must save you from having to join a gym. How much do I owe you?" I asked, still amazed at how strong Jeanine was.

Jeanine printed out my bill as I rummaged in my purse for my wallet.

After I paid for my dog's food, Jeanine said, "I know you have an appointment with Doc, but he'll be a few minutes. His brother arrived in town last night and they're in the back discussing something."

My mouth dropped open in surprise. "Jacob came home?" I hadn't seen Jacob since high school graduation. I, along with half the girls in our class had drooled over him. We high-schoolers thought him everything a captain of the football team should encompass—tall, muscular, handsome, and throw in a devastating smile that could melt your knees. Maybe we were a little jealous of Jeanine for having snagged him.

"Yes, he's here," Jeanine said. With her head bent, she flipped open another folder and made notations on it.

"Are you okay with seeing him again? I understand he's successful in real estate in Las Vegas." My curiosity piqued, I found myself self-consciously smoothing down the front of my T-shirt.

"I wouldn't know and couldn't care less," Jeanine said and slapped the folder closed.

I frowned. "I'm sorry. Did I say something wrong?" I could have bitten my tongue off. I had upset her and regretted it. She'd always been so kind to me and Porkchop whenever we visited the animal hospital. I guess not everyone got over their ex as quickly as I did mine. Apparently, she still had feelings for Jacob, whether good or bad.

"No, no. I think what happened to Calvin has rattled me." Jeanine pushed back her chair and stood. She walked over to a row of file cabinets lining the wall behind her desk. She pulled open a drawer and stuffed a file in then slammed it shut, with a little more force than I thought necessary.

I sniffed the air. My nose twitched. The smell. There it was again, the one from the shelter. Was Doc using a new disinfectant for the hospital?

The fragrance tickled my nose. I placed a hand over my mouth to stifle a sneeze. "That scent, have you changed to a new kind of cleaner? I noticed it at the shelter earlier, too."

She sighed. "No, Jacob brought a bunch of bottles from Las Vegas with him. It's some sort of cologne he's pushing. I guess you wouldn't call it unisex, but it's supposed to be for both pets and their owners. One of his get-rich schemes. He's always trying to make the fast buck. Doc said he could display a few bottles on the counter over there. I reek of it by the time I leave here in the evening." Jeanine pointed to a row of bottles at the end of the counter. A large woman with close-cropped gray hair, had come into the vet's. She spritzed herself and her pug with a tester. I didn't think Porkchop would go for matching perfumes.

Shouting erupted from behind the swinging wooden doors leading to the examination area. The door burst open and out strode Jacob Sorenson, as handsome as the day we graduated. I couldn't help it, my pulse sped up at the sight of his slicked-back blond hair. But a scowl marred his good looks. He was obviously upset about something.

"Hi, Jacob," I said as he brushed past me.

He stopped short and turned around. His eyes narrowed as if he were trying to place me.

I extended my hand to him. "Sam, Samantha Reynolds Davies. We went to Wings Falls High together."

He enfolded my hand in his. "Oh, yes I remember you. You are married to some undertaker fellow, right?" He may not have come home often, but I guess he kept up with class news.

"Was." My hand tingled at his touch.

He still held my hand in his, more like caressed. "*Was*? As in widowed, divorced?"

"Divorced, for five years now, but I am still involved in the business." He must have missed that old news flash.

A smile lit up his handsome face. "And you haven't remarried. A good-looking woman like you? I'm surprised."

Did drool stream out of the corners of my mouth? No, it couldn't have because suddenly it felt as dry as the Sahara. Was Jacob flirting with *me*? The class bookworm? I now considered myself, the former class bookworm, but still.

"Ugh!" Came from behind me.

I turned to find Jeanine bent over a computer. "Something wrong?" I asked.

"No, it must be something I ate. The baloney in my sandwich must have gone bad," she said, but she glared at Jacob.

"Sam, do you have plans for tonight? I've been in Vegas for so long, building my real estate empire, I don't know any of the good places to eat in town anymore. Wings Falls has changed so much over the years." Jacob rubbed his thumb across the back of my hand.

Jacob asking me out? My knees became weak. I leaned against the counter for support. Who was I kidding? No, of course he wasn't. He only wanted company and some good conversation for dinner. He was a stranger in town, having left so long ago. He probably wanted to catch up on all the Wings Falls gossip. "I'd love to have dinner with you. Wings Falls has several great places to eat. Anything special you'd like?"

His eyes stared into mine. "Some place casual. It's not often I can relax with all the high-pressure meetings and dinners I have to go to in Vegas."

"Do you like Italian? There's a great Italian restaurant on Glen Street. Momma Mia's."

"It sounds great. Would seven o'clock work for you?" he asked.

I nodded. "Yes."

"Fine, I will be there. Got to rush. I have a few business calls to make." He released my hand and hurried out of the vet's.

The door to the hospital closed behind him, Jeanine rose from her desk, her slim back ramrod straight. "Doc can meet with you now. He's in his office."

I pointed to my bag of Kibbles. "Is it okay if I leave it here while I talk to Doc?"

She nodded yes and pushed the door open to the examining room area where Doc waited. As I walked past her, she said, "Be careful tonight, very careful. Jacob is not who he pretends to be."

CHAPTER FOUR

———

After interviewing Doc Sorenson about his career as a veterinarian, I grabbed my bag of kibbles and headed home. I turned my Bug into my driveway and saw Candie sitting on the wooden rocker on my front porch. I knew by the speed of the rocker, as fast as a jet breaking the sound barrier, my cousin was agitated. By the frown on her face when I stepped out of my car, I gathered the person earning her displeasure must be me.

I placed the forty-pound bag of dog food I had bought at the vet's on my shoulder and climbed my porch steps. How Jeanine lifted these bags every day was beyond me. My gym was calling me. I gave Candie a friendly hello, but received an icy glare in return. In contrast, when I unlocked my front door, I was greeted by a jumping Porkchop, eager for a bowl of his fave dog food.

"Care for a mug of tea?" I asked my still silent cousin.

After a grunted yes to my offer of tea, we, along with a now fed Porkchop, headed for my bedroom with mugs in hand, the same bedroom I'd slept in while growing up. The Elvis and Donny Osmond posters of my youth looked down on us from the walls. But I had replaced my old maple bed and dresser with what I called my "cottage" look, mostly chippy-white furniture, the rage now on all the home decorating shows. I'd remove Donny and The King one of these days, but for now, they covered up a few cracks snaking up the walls. Painting was too big a task to tackle right now.

Candie, her legs tucked up under her flowing peasant skirt, sat ensconced in a wing chair in the corner of the room sipping the mug of tea I had brewed for her. The rhinestones on Candie's blouse twinkled in the sunlight streaming in from the window next to my bed. My cousin never met a rhinestone or two or twenty she didn't like. She sparkled as bright as them, too. If she liked you, you had a friend forever, but get on her bad side and like our Memaw Parker would say, she'd "jerk a knot in your tail."

While she sipped, I rummaged around in my closet trying to find something other than worn blue jeans to wear for my dinner with Jacob. I refused to call it a date.

I slipped a Roy Orbison CD into the player sitting on the nightstand next to my bed and hit the play button. I needed Roy's mellow voice to float over my frazzled nerves. They still jumped from my morning's encounter with Calvin and the police.

Candie's long, red-polished fingernails tapped the edge of her mug. "How dare you tell Jeanine Wagner about Calvin's demise before y'all told me! I had to learn about Calvin's death from Mark. And turn off that CD, it's driving me nuts."

I reached over to the nightstand and punched the CD player's off button. Candie didn't have the same appreciation I did for the late, great singer or my love for the fabulous 50s. I also included Donny amongst my faves.

She sat and watched as I flung the contents of my closet onto my rumpled bed. To say I upset her, I might as well compare Mount Everest to a molehill.

"Don't have a hissy fit. I had to go over to Doc Sorenson's after the police station. Porkchop ran out of food, and I needed to interview Doc for an article I'm writing on his career. Anyway, Gladys called and told her about Calvin before I even got to the vet's." I held a V-neck black silk blouse in front of me and turned for Candie's inspection. "I'm having dinner with Doc's brother, Jacob Sorenson, tonight. Is this top too sexy?"

"I'm not having a hissy fit. It's escalating to a duck fit." Candie frowned and shook her head. "And no, it is not too sexy. In fact, I don't think you even own a sexy outfit."

Oh, geez, she had neared the duck fit stage. A duck fit is the Southern equivalent of a major meltdown. I hoped it didn't get to a dying duck fit, then Porkchop and I both had better dive under my bed, if I could find it beneath all the clothes piled on top.

"So, tell me everything I missed this morning, and don't you dare leave out one detail. Then maybe I will forgive you for not calling me after you left the shelter. Well, maybe after your visit to the police station." Candie took a sip of her chamomile tea, but the soothing qualities of the tea weren't working on her.

I pushed aside a pile of clothes I had thrown onto my bed, sat down, and began my saga. I had repeated it so many times to the police, more specifically Detective Johnson, I could repeat it in my dreams, or should, I say nightmares. "Okay, minding my own business, I drove over to Calvin's pet shelter. You know, trying to do a good deed, when I, well should I say Porkchop, stumbled onto Calvin's body."

After Candie listened to my tale she leaned back in the wing chair. "You said a car squealed out of the parking lot when you got there." She cradled the mug in her hands, hopefully finally calming down.

"Yes, and Gladys mentioned Frank Gilbert supposedly went to meet with Calvin about donating to the shelter. You don't think Frank saw the murderer, do you?" I pulled my dog onto my lap. He'd nestled into the clothes that had slid off my bed onto the floor. At times like these, he was better than a security blanket. His warm body gave me comfort.

Candie dropped her legs to the floor and sat upright in the chair. "Frank drove to the shelter? Did you tell the police?"

"I don't know for sure he did. I didn't see the car with my eyes. I only saw a cloud of dust, and I didn't want to get him in trouble." I stroked Porkchop's fur. I hoped to transfer his calm energy into me. "Gladys tried to reach him on her iPhone. Did you know she has one?"

"Not get him into trouble! Sam, we're talking about a murder investigation. He could be the murderer. Every bit of evidence becomes important. Mark would be the first one to tell you how important." The way the sequins on her blouse bounced, I feared her duck fit had returned.

"But Candie, he's such a sweet man. He wouldn't hurt a flea. You know how he takes care of the animals down at Doc's place and the good work he does at the shelter. I couldn't imagine him harming anyone. Anyway, I didn't know he went AWOL from Gladys's phone until I talked to her." I turned my best sad eyes on Candie.

"I'm sure Lizzie Borden acted like a sweet girl, too, until she finished whacking her parents." Candie shook her head. She pushed one of the auburn curls framing her freckled face out of her violet eyes. Memaw Parker had said she looked like one of those Gibson Girls from the turn of the century. The nineteenth century I mean. She had generous high breasts and a tiny waist to die for, with hips great for birth'n babies. In a word, my cousin looked gorgeous.

"Candie, puleease. I need help. I haven't had dinner with someone I looked forward to being with since I don't know when. I'm dining with Jacob Sorenson. You know, the hunk I'd write you about when we were in high school. The guy who at least ninety-nine percent of the senior class girls crushed on in high school. Do you think my black Levi's will go with this top? They hug my buns real nice if I do say so myself." I placed my dog on the floor and rummaged through the clothes stacked on my bed for the jeans I knew accentuated one of my best assets.

Candie furrowed her brow. "Yes, they'll look great, especially if you wear your high-heeled boots with them. And what do you mean you haven't looked forward to a dinner since you don't know when? What about the dates from the *Dates 4 U* I set you up with? I thought you said they were memorable."

"Oh, yes, memorable would describe them. How can I forget my date with Herb, the computer programmer? You know, the guy who thought he programmed me into existence on his computer and acted as my program master. And how about Peter? The guy who brought his pet tarantula into the restaurant and unbeknownst to me, fed it grasshoppers all through dinner. I wanted to gag." Why couldn't Candie accept the fact that I considered being single was okay? I flicked my Levi's to look for wrinkles and if I would need to pull out the dreaded ironing board.

Candie nodded and smiled. "I guess you were right about those two fellows, but you have to admit you didn't find out about the tarantula until the grasshoppers escaped Peter's pocket and started hopping all over the table. He did keep the spider hidden under the table until it was time for dessert."

"I don't do spiders either on or off dates. You know I have this thing about those icky creatures. They send me screaming out of a room." I decided on the V-neck silk blouse and black Levi's then started to re-hang the mess covering my bed and half of the bedroom floor.

Candie laughed. "I can imagine you screaming and running from the restaurant. Guess you didn't have another date with him."

I rolled my eyes towards the ceiling. "Thank heavens I have caller ID. I never answered when he tried to call me."

"At least you are excited about your date with Jacob. Didn't Jeanine date him in high school? I remember you saying they made a hot couple back then." Candie reached down and handed me a pink blouse that had slipped to the floor.

"Yes, but I guess, like most high school romances, it did not last after they went away to college. And this isn't a date. We are two people having dinner together." I had finally made up my mind. The Levi's looked fine, no wrinkles, and hung them on a hanger over the doorknob to my closet. I didn't want them to get swallowed up in the chaos on my bed. I shook my head and silently chastised myself. Why was I so concerned about a few wrinkles? It's not like this was a real date.

"It's hard to make long-distance romances work," Candie said.

"True, but I think more happened than a romance from thirty years ago fizzling out." I smiled at Porkchop curled amid the clothes on my bed, snoring softly. "Today at Doc's place when I mentioned Jacob to her, if looks could kill, I swear Calvin wouldn't be the only one in the morgue. Jacob would be his roomie."

Candie set her mug on a small table next to the wing chair. "Maybe she didn't like him dumping her. You said she loved him more than a cat loves cream."

"I thought so at the time, but I think more is involved. Over thirty years have passed since we graduated from high school. I would think she'd get over her high school flame by now." I hated to disturb Porkchop, who lay curled up in the pile of clothes on the bed, but I wanted to clean up my room before I left in a few hours to meet Jacob.

Candie stood and handed me her mug. "Well, I'd better scoot so you can get ready for your date. What time do you meet him at Momma Mia's?"

"I told you it's not a date. Anyway, I'm meeting him at seven. I know he'll love Brian's cooking." Brian Mayfield wasn't Italian, but he made the best lasagna this side of Italy.

"I hear you." Candie laughed and waved her ringed fingers as she left me to straighten my bedroom.

* * *

"Beautiful night, isn't it?"

Startled by the voice behind me, I jumped.

I was sitting on a wooden park bench outside Momma Mia's waiting for Jacob. It was a lovely night to observe the people that meandered down Glen Street. The night air became a little cool for the end of August. This morning's weather forecast was off by several degrees. The high had only reached the low eighties and the temperature was dropping now as night began to fall. I tugged the soft black sweater I brought with me tighter around my shoulders.

"I'm sorry. Didn't mean to give you a heart attack."

"Oh, hi Patsy. I'm okay, a little on edge I guess." Patsy Ikeda, a fellow "hooker" and member of the Loopy Ladies was a second-generation Japanese American. Seventyish and slender, her gray-streaked black hair skimmed her shoulders. She and her dog, Hana, a Japanese Spitz, stood next to the bench.

"Hello, Hana. How are you doing this evening?" I bent to stroke his long white fur and gave him a scratch between his pointy ears. His curled tail flopped against his back. Patsy claimed his breed was one of Japan's "national treasures." I knew Hana meant everything to her.

"I understand you discovered Calvin's body this morning." Patsy gave Hana's leash a gentle tug. On cue, he sat at his mistress's feet.

I blinked and stared at Patsy. "How did you know?"

"Got a call from Gladys. Can't say I will miss the man. If anything, whoever killed him did the world a favor. He never did anything if it didn't benefit him. He'd find a way to get his hooks into you and bleed you dry. Come on Hana, we'd better finish our walk. See you at Loopy Ladies Monday morning." Before I could respond, Patsy tugged on Hana's leash, and they continued their stroll down the sidewalk.

I double blinked as they walk away. Patsy nodded as she passed people she knew. The long fur of Hana's tail gently waved in the night breeze. What did Patsy have against Calvin

Perkins? Why would she want him dead? And why would Gladys think his death would interest Patsy Ikeda? Since she and Gladys were close friends, maybe Gladys just thought Patsy would want to know the latest town gossip. Gladys's iPhone must have burned with the info on Calvin.

* * *

Jacob pulled out my chair. "Did you have any trouble finding the place?" I asked.

"Sorry I am late. I had a last-minute call about a real estate deal I'm working on in Vegas. I remember this place from my youth, but it wasn't an Italian restaurant then. I think a bicycle repair shop operated here." Jacob seated himself across from me.

I'd warmed the bench outside Momma Mia's until seven thirty. I'd started to think Jacob wasn't going to show when I saw him saunter down the street like he didn't have a care in the world. A slow burn had crept up my neck, but when he finally came to a stop in front of me, he pulled a box of chocolates from behind his back. A smile spread across my face. "You do know the way to a girl's heart. Or at least mine. Chocolate makes up for any tardiness." All was forgiven.

Wax dripped down a candle stuck in the Chianti bottle in the middle of the red-checkered cloth covering our table. Perry Como crooned over the din of the diners. People packed the restaurant. Thank heavens I had called earlier and made a reservation. The candlelight reflected in Jacob's brown eyes, eyes wanting to pull me in. I could understand why he had become so successful. When he looked at you, the rest of the world melted away.

He flipped open his napkin and spread it across his lap. "You look lovely tonight. How was your day?"

My face grew warm under his gaze. It had been a long time since a member of the opposite sex had paid me a compliment, and I liked it. "I guess you know about Calvin Perkins and how I found him lying on the floor at the shelter. I do not think I will ever forget the image of his dead body." A shiver passed through my body as I recalled the moment. I picked up the fork sitting next to my plate and flipped it between my fingers. Was I nervous about eating dinner with Jacob or more upset by Calvin's death than I realized?

Jacob reached across the table and took my hand. "Did you notice anyone else there when you arrived at the shelter?"

"No, but I do remember hearing a car leave the parking lot." I must call Detective Johnson tomorrow and tell him this, I mentally chided myself.

Jacob's eyes narrowed and his hand tightened on mine. "You do? Did you see it?"

"Ouch." I pulled my hand from his and rubbed it. What had made him squeeze my hand so tightly?

"Sorry, I didn't mean to hurt you." Jacob's lopsided smile begged me to forgive him.

"Jacob, Jacob Sorenson, you thief, I'm surprised you have the guts to show your face in town after what you did to me."

I gazed up and found Gladys and her errant beau, Frank Gilbert, standing next to our table. Frank's face was redder than one of Memaw's prize tomatoes. He shook a gnarled finger at Jacob. Gladys tugged on the sleeve of his flannel shirt. She tried to gently lead him away from our table. Diners stopped eating and looked towards the commotion. Silence descended on the restaurant.

I frowned and glanced at Jacob or attempted to. A large plastic-coated menu hid his face. "What was Frank so angry about?"

Jacob lowered the menu and glared at Frank and Gladys's retreating backs. "Nothing for you to worry about. Let's order dinner." He motioned for a waitress to come over to our table.

"My spaghetti was fabulous. How was your lasagna?" It was all I could do not to groan—I was so full.

Jacob took a sip of wine. He'd ordered my favorite Riesling to have with our dinner. "Great recommendation. Next time I'm back in town I'll definitely dine here again."

"Did Brian's cooking live up to your Las Vegas standards?" I laid down my fork and reached for the glass of wine I'd sipped throughout our meal. Brian had outdone himself.

"He'd give any of those casino chefs a run for their money. Glad you recommended the lasagna. Best I've ever tasted." Jacob placed his napkin on the table and leaned back in his chair.

The night had been filled with a walk down memory lane. We'd recalled the highlights and lowlights of our high school years. He talked about his football glory days and his exciting life in Las Vegas. But the early encounter Jacob had with Frank still niggled at me.

I took a sip of wine, then threw out the question still bothering me. "Why was Frank so upset with you? I have never noticed him so angry before. He's usually such an even-tempered man."

"You know, every Vegas deal I make isn't a sure thing. You have to pull your big boy pants on when you're hanging with the high rollers in that town. Calvin, the old skinflint, wanted to get in on the ground floor of a transaction I was making. He convinced Frank to invest money, too. It didn't pan out. They lost a few dollars. Why get mad at me? I didn't twist Frank's arm to fork over his money. If anything, maybe he shouldn't have listened to Calvin."

Jacob's eyes clouded over. A frown marred his handsome face. "Frank's got nerve accosting me like he did. Maybe he was still mad at Calvin for losing money and he killed Calvin. Gladys should check on where her wandering boyfriend went this morning."

My brain jolted into overdrive. *What does Jacob know about Frank's whereabouts this morning? Was he at For Pet's Sake this morning, too?*

CHAPTER FIVE

―――――

"Decaf, Sam? And Candie, none of this chicken brew for you, right?" Franny clenched two coffeepots in her smooth brown hands, one pot banded in orange for the decaf and the other containing regular coffee.

Candie nodded towards the dark handled pot and lifted her mug to Franny Goodway for a fill-up. "You've got what I need, a dose of some good caffeine."

Candie and I sat in a booth in Sweetie Pie's Café for our weekly helping of Southern comfort food after Saint Anthony's Sunday, ten o'clock Mass.

"Sam?" Franny pointed the orange-rimmed coffeepot at me.

"I guess so." I eyed Candie with envy as she sipped her delicious caffeine-packed nectar. The aroma of freshly ground coffee beans made my mouth water. My doctor had relegated me to decaf ever since my blood pressure started to go north, while I fought to keep the rest of my body from plunging south.

I slid my coffee mug across the worn red Formica tabletop towards Franny. Candie and I sat in our usual booth, next to a window that looked out on Main Street. Franny had opened Sweetie Pie's fifteen years ago, after she moved north from Alabama. You'd never know by her rail-thin figure that she ranked as one of Wings Falls' best cooks. From the first day she flipped over the open sign in the café's front window and began to serve up her Southern comfort food, it had topped Wings Falls' list as a top ten favorite. Franny served home-style comfort food, nothing fancy, but plentiful and delicious. Food that reminded me of my summers spent with Candie on Memaw Parker's farm in Hainted Holler, Tennessee. Memaw would serve up chicken-fried steak with a side of her fabulous sweet potato casserole. If Candie and I had been especially good she'd end the dinner with a serving of fresh peach cobbler topped with a scoop of vanilla ice cream. My mouth watered thinking about Memaw's cooking. The café décor didn't boast anything elaborate, either. It reminded me of a 50s diner. Booths hugged three glossy white walls. A checkerboard pattern of black and white tiles covered the floor. A counter and red vinyl upholstered stools fronted the kitchen wall. As usual, patrons occupied each of the five stools. If you didn't look too closely, you wouldn't notice Sweetie Pie's worn edges. A few of the booths' benches sported duct tape to mend rips, and the waitresses served your meals on mismatched but spotless dinnerware.

All of this only added to Sweetie Pie's charm. Franny prided herself in the café's cleanliness and her great cooking. So, what did a few worn floor tiles and some duct tape matter? I scanned the restaurant and waved to the diners I knew, which included most everyone. Did the topic of this morning's gossip include my stumbling across Calvin's body yesterday? Especially, with Gladys fueling the gossip line. I would bet a new designer handbag it did.

"You want this morning's special?" Franny lifted her chin towards the chalkboard hanging behind the counter. Tight black curls caressed her head. White chalk spelled out the special dishes Franny offered her customers today.

Candie squinted at the board. Glasses weren't too far off for her. I had told her for months to make an appointment to get her eyes checked. "Looks good to me," she said. "How'd ja know I hankered for the ham and eggs this morning?"

We all laughed. Any meal remotely Southern "looked good" to Candie.

Candie and Franny trained their eyes on me. Not a difficult choice for me. I ate the same thing every Sunday morning—a bowl of grits topped with a pat of butter and a side of bacon.

"My usual," I said, taking a sip of my coffee.

Franny and Candie laughed again. "You sure have become predictable," Franny said. "I knew you would order grits and bacon even before you sat down. I will be back soon with your breakfast." Franny pulled an order pad out of the pocket of the short black apron tied around her slim waist. She jotted down our order then turned and walked towards the kitchen humming "Amazing Grace."

I frowned then squinted at Candie. "I'm not *that* predictable, am I?"

Candie looked up from stirring three packets of sugar into her coffee. She laid the spoon on the table. "Let's say no one will ever call you wild and crazy."

I pressed my spine against the back of the booth's bench seat. "Because I haven't had the most, how shall I put it, diverse love life like you, does not make me dull. I can be wild and throw in some crazy, too." Yeah, right, my parents would choke on their evening cocktails if their staid little Samantha did anything wild. "I will show you. Next time I might order home fries, or maybe even…" I wrinkled my forehead and tried to think of something daring. "Or one of Franny's cinnamon buns. Yeah, I will order one of those." I pointed to the saucer-sized mound of deliciousness, dripping with frosting, sitting on the counter under a plastic dome. If I ever dared to eat one of those buns, I'd have to spend an extra hour a day for a week on the treadmill at the gym running off the calories. Although, come to think of it, grits and a side of bacon were not exactly diet food.

"A cinnamon bun?" Candie shook her head and rolled her eyes. "You are pathetic." She knew my acting 'wild and crazy' was as likely to happen as her cat, Dixie, and my Porkchop becoming BFFs.

I leaned over the table and flipped through the song selection cards in the tabletop jukebox. A mini jukebox sat on the end of the table in each booth filled with my kind of music, 50s hits. I unzipped my handbag, a red Isaac Mizrahi with an all-over blue peacock feather design. I pulled out my wallet and dug some quarters out of the change compartment.

My hand poised over the jukebox, clutching two quarters. "So, what do you want to listen to this morning?"

Candie shrugged her shoulders. The only thing she didn't like about having Sunday breakfast with me was my selection of fave music. I loved eating Sunday breakfast while listening to Elvis, Roy, and maybe the Big Bopper. Maybe I'd get her dander up and throw in some Donny. Like me, Franny loved Donny and had a few of his records added to the jukebox mix.

I flipped through the selection cards of the jukebox. "You know you swoon over the music by your Memphis boy, Elvis."

Candie sighed and set down her coffee. "I guess if you put it in such a way, I am obligated to fulfill my Southern duty and listen to him."

I smiled. I knew she was a closet Elvis lover, even if she wouldn't admit it. I fed quarters into the mini jukebox and punched in E5 for "Can't Help Falling in Love."

"Here you go, ladies."

I jumped. I hadn't noticed Franny standing next to our table, our breakfast plates lined up her thin arm. I never could figure out how she balanced all those plates and not drop one. I'd be a disaster as a waitress.

"Thanks so much, Franny." I pressed against the back of the booth so she could set down our meal.

She nodded at our half-empty mugs. "Want a refill?"

I tipped my mug towards me and examined what remained. "Sure, if it's not too much of a bother."

Franny scooted behind the counter and retrieved the coffeepots. She topped off our coffee and told us to "Enjoy" then hurried off to take care of more of the Sunday-morning-after-church rush.

"So, tell me all about your date with Jacob," Candie said while slicing her ham.

She hung on to my last night's dinner with Jacob like white on rice. "I told you we ate dinner and talked about old times and life since high school, nothing more."

"Whatever. Give me the details." Candie dug her fork into the eggs.

Between spoonfuls of grits, I told her about my evening. Besides sharing Jacob and my trip down memory lane, I told her about the great meal Brian had prepared.

"But the strangest thing that happened was how Frank reacted to Jacob. Gladys had to hold Frank back to keep him from clobbering Jacob. I mean, I didn't notice any love lost between the two of them. When I asked Jacob about Frank, he fluffed it off and said it was sour grapes about some Las Vegas deal gone bad. He said Calvin was in on it, too. And speaking of no love lost, I met Patsy Ikeda while I waited for Jacob. She strolled by walking the beautiful dog of hers, Hana. She didn't have anything pleasant to say about Calvin, either. She mentioned that he used people. And to quote her 'once he got his hooks into you, he'd bleed you dry.' She sounded like she spoke from personal experience. Do you think he knew something about her she didn't want made public? He may not be the most popular man in town, but I think she is positively happy he is dead."

Candie sipped her coffee and frowned. Morning sunlight streamed in from the windows and sparkled off the gems on her ringed fingers. "You are right, not many people cared for him, but to die like that in such a horrible way, whacked in the head with a dog bone? I cannot imagine it. Whoever hit him had to have a pretty good 'arm.'"

I shivered, remembering Calvin sprawled out on the shelter floor. Bags of kibble covered his body. Porkchop lay nearby, his tail wagging while he gnawed on the murder weapon.

Candie placed her mug of coffee on the table and looked at me. "Doesn't Patsy pitch for the senior center softball team?"

Candie's question yanked me back to the present. "What? Oh, yeah. In fact, she's the senior league champion. I hear she practices all year. She has a setup in her basement so she can keep her pitching arm in shape even in the off-season." I took another sip of my coffee.

Candie leaned across the table and whispered, "You don't think she could have—you know? Especially if she thought of Calvin as a mean ol' egg-sucking dawg 'with his hooks' in her."

I didn't understand what she meant. "What?" I asked.

Candie huffed out a stream of air that caused the bangs on her forehead to flutter. "Geez, do I have to spell it out to you? A minute ago, you said Patsy practically did the happy dance since Calvin is deader than a doornail."

"Candie." Calvin may not have won the town's best-loved citizen award. In fact, little love flowed his way, but the dead deserved a little respect. Guess it came from all my years as a partner in a funeral home business.

She dabbed at the corner of her mouth with a paper napkin. "Okay, okay, but do you think she could have been the one to, umm, do him in?"

I stared at my coffee. Did Patsy dislike Calvin so much she could have killed him? She acted happy to hear he had died. And if what Candie said was true, that someone with a good 'arm' must have killed him, then it would put her in the running as a prime suspect. But, Patsy? Petite, Patsy? I shook my head. I couldn't believe it, not her. But stranger things have happened, I guess. Why did she dislike him so much? Was there something in her past that she wanted kept secret and Calvin knew about it? She had never uttered an unkind word about anyone, even at Loopy Ladies where the gossip mill worked overtime.

"Thanks, Hank."

My head snapped up at Franny's mention of the detective's name. Sure enough, Detective Johnson stood by the cash register at the end of the counter. He clutched some bills in his hand for a takeout drink Franny had handed him. When did he enter the café? Candie and I had been so busy talking about Calvin's murder, I hadn't noticed him come in. He turned to leave when his eyes met mine. Drat, why did my heart do a little hip-hop? What was wrong with me? Last night I drooled over Jacob. The detective nodded, and I smiled in return.

"Great," I said to myself, as he walked towards us. I wanted to slide under the booth.

"What's wrong?" Candie must have noticed my deer-caught-in-the-headlights expression.

"Nothing. Everything," I mumbled. Why was I reacting like this to Detective Johnson? Even in the early days of my relationship with my ex, George, I had never felt so flustered and giddy. I snatched a menu from behind the metal napkin holder at the end of our table, then studied it as if engrossed in the greatest novel ever published. I was guilty of repeating Jacob's performance from last night when he'd encountered Frank Gilbert.

"Morning, ladies."

Hank, in all his handsomeness, stood next to our table. The blue of his denim shirt matched the blue in his eyes—eyes that made my heart race. Or maybe I was suffering from a heart attack. At fifty-five, I was in the prime heart attack age group or so the pamphlets sitting next to the three-year-old magazines in my doctor's office reminded me. Jeans hugged his muscled thighs. By his casual clothes I guessed he was off duty, no tie or suit jacket today.

I lowered the menu. "Hello, Detective Johnson." Candie kicked me under the table. "Oh, yes, let me introduce my cousin, Candie."

He extended a calloused hand towards Candie. She enfolded it in her long, slender fingers.

"My pleasure, Detective, sir. I heard you are new in town and have to deal with all the nasty Calvin Perkins business."

I swear she blushed and batted her eyes at him. I returned her kick.

"Ouch!" Candie reached under the table to rub her shin.

His baby blues bore into my green eyes. "Yes, ma'am, you heard right. I imagine from your cousin here."

Now it was my turn to blush. "Guilty as charged."

"A hummm." Candie jerked her head towards Detective Johnson.

I frowned. Had my cousin suddenly developed a nervous tic and needed medical attention? We could call 9-1-1 and share an ambulance ride to the hospital, she for her tic and me for my racing heart. Then I understood what she wanted— for me to tell the detective about the noise I'd heard when I arrived at the shelter.

I fiddled with my mug. "Umm, Detective."

A smile curved his lips. "Hank, please."

"Yes, well, Hank, I remembered something about when I arrived at the shelter."

He glanced at the stainless-steel watch on his left wrist. "I have an appointment in about ten minutes that I can't rearrange. Can you come by the station in the morning, and I will add it to your statement? You'll have to initial it."

"Can I stop by in the afternoon? I have some hooking I want to finish." I thought of the rug on my frame my fingers itched to tackle. Besides, I wasn't about to jump at his command. Well, maybe his request.

Hank cocked one of his well-shaped eyebrows at me.

I laughed. "I mean rug hooking. We rug makers get into the habit of shortening our name and never give it a thought."

"I understand, but I suggest you turn your menu right side up. It might be easier to read." He gave us a two-fingered salute and turned to walk out of the café.

I smacked my forehead with the palm of my hand. How stupid of me to have the menu upside down when trying to hide behind it. He had to know I wanted to avoid him.

Candie stared out the door after Hank. "You didn't tell me he was so handsome. If I wasn't dating Mark, I'd love to be the butter melting all over his pancakes."

"Candie, are you crazy? He must be ten years younger than us. Why I'm practically old enough to be his...big sister." I shook my head and tried to clear it of any thoughts of Hank Johnson.

"Big sister, my foot. Why I was older than, let me think." Candie   tapped her chin with her fingernail. "I was older than fiancés number three and nine. I found my experiences positively helpful. Oh my, look who walked in."

My head swiveled towards the door. Shirley Carrigan stood in the doorway, Calvin Perkins' live-in girlfriend for the past five years. She did not look the part of a grieving girlfriend—no puffy, bloodshot eyes from hours of crying. She waved a cheery hello to a fellow diner.

CHAPTER SIX

————

I always thought Shirley and Calvin had made an odd couple. She was tall, at least five-foot-seven, and well-toned, to his short five-foot-three and overweight by at least fifty pounds. He'd come across as loud and abrasive while she always hung in the background, quiet, at least when around him. I knew she worked out at Fitness World because I'd seen her there whenever I got the guilts and thought I should do something about my neglected body. She stood in the doorway of Sweetie Pie's dressed like she'd come fresh from a workout: black skin-tight capri yoga pants, a sleeveless neon green tank top, and sneakers. I don't think most men would call her a beauty, because of her offset nose and large build, but she was pleasant-looking. Her chestnut brown hair dangled down her back in a thick braid, and women would die for her creamy smooth skin.

I called her name as she walked by our booth. "I'm sorry about Calvin." Talk about feeling awkward. I knew I should say something, but I felt like I had done the "deed."

"Don't give it another thought," she said. She bounced from one foot to another. Guess she hadn't come out of her workout mode. "It was bound to happen sooner or later. I'm surprised no one killed him sooner."

"Huh?" I nearly dropped the mug I had raised halfway to my lips. I looked across the table at Candie, but she shook her head. Candie must know something about Shirley and Calvin's relationship that she hadn't shared with me. Her large hoop earrings swayed back and forth.

Shirley waggled her fingers at us. "Scoot over."

I moved closer to the window to make room for her as she slid onto the booth's bench seat. She looked over her shoulder and waved to Franny who was waiting on the table next to ours.

Once Franny had finished with the next table's order, she walked over to us. "What can I get ya'll?" Franny, like Candie, even after all these years living up north, still hung on to her Southern accent.

Shirley wrinkled up her forehead as if considering a twenty-million-dollar question. "I will start off with a steaming mug of coffee, but let me think for a minute about what I want to eat. Can't make up my mind between a stack of blueberry pancakes or some of your biscuits and gravy."

Franny poked a pencil behind her ear. "One coffee coming up. Take your time deciding. I'm not going anywhere." She chuckled then strode off to the counter to fetch the coffeepot and a mug.

I smelled it again. A cinnamon scent, the one I'd first detected at the shelter when I discovered Calvin's body, then again at Doc's office, also last night when I talked to Patsy, and while I ate dinner with Jacob. Was I the only one in town not wearing this perfume? Or did the perfume have a link to Calvin's murderer? Was the murderer wearing the perfume?

Shirley turned back to us and leaned her elbows on the table. "Whoever killed Calvin did me a favor. Many a time I would have loved to do him in myself." Her hands flew to her mouth as she gave us a startled look. "Oh, I'm not saying I killed him. No, no. I couldn't have done such a terrible thing. I am only saying I should have left the bum five years ago." She snatched a napkin from the metal holder at the end of the table and started to shred it. Bits of paper fluttered to the table in front of her. Why was she so nervous? Was her explanation a feeble attempt on her part to excuse herself as a possible murder suspect?

"I didn't know things were so bad between you and Calvin. Were the two of you going to break up?" Maybe they got in an argument at the animal shelter and things got out of hand. His murder could have been an accident. Maybe in the heat of the moment Shirley hit him with the dog bone. She certainly looked strong enough to give him a good whack.

Her muscled shoulders shuddered. "I'm sorry you had to find him. It couldn't have been pleasant."

Franny arrived back with the coffeepot and a mug for Shirley. She filled it, then nodded towards Candie and me. "You ladies want a refill?" She pointed the coffeepot at us.

I patted my stomach and tried to stifle a groan. "I don't think I could swallow another thing."

My cousin lifted her mug to Franny. "You can top me off." I'd never known her to refuse more coffee. I swear coffee ran in her veins.

"Hey, Franny, can I have a refill while you're dishing some out?" a customer at the counter yelled.

"Hold your horses. I will be right with you. Can't you see I am busy?" Franny shook her head and rolled her eyes at us. "Some days I ask myself why I turn my *Open* sign over."

The three of us laughed. I knew even with a demanding customer every once in a while, Franny would not have things any other way. Sweetie Pie's had become her life.

When Franny walked away to wait on her coffee-deprived customer, I turned to Shirley. "Can't say finding Calvin was the best way to start my day. Why did you stay with him for so long if you didn't care for him?" Maybe I'm too independent, but once I found out what a louse George was, I could not get Porkchop and myself out of the house fast enough.

A strange look passed between Candie and Shirley. What did their eye messages mean? What secrets did they share?

"Caring for him or not had nothing to do with it. Sometimes you do things you don't exactly want to do. We're not all lucky like you, Sam. You had Candie to run to when you split from your ex. Where would I go?" Shirley grabbed her mug and abruptly stood. She walked over to the counter and sat on one of the stools. She picked a menu off the counter and stared at it as if she needed to commit Sweetie Pie's offerings to memory for a test before she could order.

"Lucky? Me lucky? She had nerve to say I was lucky. I've worked hard building a new life for myself after George wrecked our marriage. And what did I say to make her spandex twist into such a knot?" I clutched the mug handle in a death grip. My temper started to shoot upward. "And what about the look darting between the two of you?"

The coffee in Candie's mug suddenly became extremely interesting to her. Would the grounds at the bottom of the mug reveal the future to her? If she thought ignoring me would put me off, she had another think coming.

I tried to nudge her into answering me. "Candie."

She looked up at me from under long eyelashes. "I can't say much. She came to the women's shelter a few times. I'm sure you can guess at the reasons why women come there. Abuse, both physical and mental, is one of the main reasons. I can't go into any detail as to why Shirley came. But knowing the kind of person Calvin was, you can come to your own conclusions. Did you know she once wrestled for the WWF?"

I knew Candie volunteered at the town's women's shelter three days a week. Even though she and I had few secrets between us, I also knew what went on at the shelter remained strictly confidential.

I frowned. "The WWF? What is it?"

"The Women's Wrestling Federation," she said.

"You mean like Hulk Hogan or Haystack Calhoun?" Grandpa Parker had loved wrestling. I'd spent most of my summers while visiting Candie in Hainted Holler, Tennessee— with him and Memaw Parker. Every Saturday afternoon he'd stretch out on his old recliner with patched armrests and turn on the wrestling matches. He would wave his gnarled fist at the TV, shout at his favorite wrestler, and call down dire consequences if they lost.

"Yes, but only with female wrestlers. She made a big name for herself during her wrestling career. I believe her professional name was Shirley the Slammer."

"She was pretty happy Calvin has died. I didn't notice any blood-shot or puffy eyes, as if she had been crying over the death of her boyfriend. I think she works out regularly at the gym. I've seen her lifting weights a bunch of times when I've gone there. She'd have what you called a 'good arm.' Do you think she could have killed him?" Could Shirley the Slammer have slammed the bone into Calvin's skull? I grossed myself out. My grits performed somersaults in my stomach.

"I don't know, but I think we had better get going. There's a line at the door for seats." Candie nodded towards the café's door. A line of customers waiting to be seated snaked out onto the sidewalk.

I motioned to Franny for our check. On Sundays, we took turns paying the bill. Today was Candie's turn to pay, and I'd leave the tip.

I slipped my wallet out of my purse. "Yeah, Calvin's murder makes it hard to concentrate. I have got to get to work on the article I'm writing. I need to give Jeanine a call in the morning and ask if I can meet with the Doc one more time. He's been terribly generous with his time, but I have a few more questions before I can wrap it up and hit *Send*." I placed a five on the table under my coffee mug then slid out of our booth.

"Speaking of phone calls, don't forget to give your hunky Hank a call tomorrow, too." A grin spread across Candie's face. "Hunky Hank, I like it. Really describes him."

I put a finger to my lips. "Shhhh, will you be quiet? Someone could hear you. He's not my Hunky Hank, and I'm going to stop by the station after Loopy Ladies tomorrow." I grabbed Candie's elbow and tried to hurry her out of the café without bumping into a busy waitress or two.

Candie laughed. "Okay, okay, but he sure acted interested in you."

I edged her towards the door. "Right, you could tell he was interested from witnessing our two-minute conversation."

"I know about these things. Remember I've had a lot of practice."

I wasn't going to dispute Candie about her knowledge regarding the male population. I had only known one man in my lifetime, my ex, and my marriage had ended in a big bust, but on this I thought she was all wrong.

We waved to Franny on the way out, but Shirley didn't turn an inch on her stool when we walked by. Her head bent over her plate, she dug into her flapjacks and ate them like they were her last meal. As we passed her, my nose twitched with a whiff of the spicy perfume Jacob had brought from Las Vegas. Could he have been at the shelter yesterday morning? Again, I thought, maybe this was a link to the murderer. But what about Patsy and her Calvin having his hooks in a person comment. Was that person her? Or, heaven forbid, what if Frank blamed Calvin for his investing in Jacob's Las Vegas deal?

As my Southern cousin would say, the list of suspects for Calvin Perkins' murder grew faster than a tick on a hound dog.

CHAPTER SEVEN

———

"Ouch!" I rubbed my shin as I elbowed open the door to The Ewe and Me. Rug hooking was not a craft for the faint of heart. My red canvas tote had gouged me in the leg. It held all the paraphernalia for hooking my latest rug—wooden frame, scissors, wool strips, and pattern. My purse of choice today, a large black leather Michael Kors, slid down my arm.

I pushed the strap back up my arm and nudged myself into The Ewe.

"Let me help you." Bejeweled fingers reached out to retrieve the plate of brownies I balanced in my free hand. When a Loopy Lady finished one of her projects, she brought her rug plus a treat to share with the group. Today, I would proudly display my latest finished masterpiece, a small rug I had hooked of a red truck, the bed overflowing with pumpkins. A nice addition to my fall décor, I thought.

"Candie, you are a lifesaver." My cousin had joined the Loopy Ladies a few years ago, but she did more gabbing than hooking at our Monday morning get-togethers. I think her interests lay more in the type of hooking she wrote about in her romance novels than the kind that involved pulling wool strips.

"Yum, these brownies smell delicious. You must have baked them this morning."

I nodded and followed her into the studio. The studio sat behind Lucy's main show room where she sold her fabulous wool and patterns. "The doughboy and I had an early morning date."

Candie laughed. She was well acquainted with my limited abilities in the kitchen. I placed my canvas bag on the floor next to the long oak table we all gathered around to hook. Then retrieved the plate from Candie and walked into Lucy's dye room where I set the brownies next to a coffeepot gurgling away on the counter.

When I returned to the room we used for our Monday morning hook-ins, several ladies sat bent over their frames. The room we met in for our meetings had cubbies and pieces of antique furniture that held lengths of wool for our rug hooking. The old oak library table we gathered around gave us plenty of room to spread out all the equipment needed to work on our patterns. The best thing though? The windows. They lined one wall and let in plenty of sunlight to augment the overhead lights. That made this a great room for us to pull loops.

Over the years many of the twelve ladies who made up our group had become more than friends to me. We shared good times and bad, laughter and tears. They became my rock during those dark days when I found out about George's betrayal. Were some of them odd ducks? Sure, but I think we all acted a little strange in our own way.

I waved to the group. "Morning."

Mornings and hellos floated about the room.

"Ladies, before we begin can I run an idea past you?" Candie reached into her tote and pulled out an iPad. She often sought the group's advice on her romance novels, and today was no exception. "Okay, should the opening sentence of *Hot Night in Paradise* read 'Camille's breasts heaved at his touch' or 'Camille's breasts trembled at his touch'?"

Giggles filled the studio. The ladies, young and old, loved to contribute their ideas to Candie's romances, especially since she always listed them on the credit page of her books.

"Let's have a vote." Jane Burrows, our ever-organized town librarian, piped up. "Those in favor of 'heaving breasts' raise their hands." Seven hands shot into the air. Jane nodded— her pixie-cut hair didn't move an inch.

"Heaving breasts it is, then." Candie's fingers tapped this on her iPad.

"Sam, what did you observe? Tell us everything you saw, and don't leave out a thing," said Helen Garber, a hook poised over her rug. Helen was one of the more outspoken Loopy Ladies. Not much held back her tongue. Discreet was not part of her vocabulary. Subtle didn't extend to her wardrobe, either. The brighter and bolder the color, she wore it. Today she paired large red poppy-patterned slacks with a bright orange blouse.

I dragged my frame and rug out of my bag. "Drat." Hundreds of little needles surrounded the frame to grip a rug pattern to it. I had scraped a finger against them. "What?" I mumbled around my finger. I sucked at my cut to stop the flow of blood. Helen's sudden change of topic had taken me by surprise.

"I was told you arrived first on the scene of Calvin Perkins' grizzly murder. Is it true a river of blood covered the floor and his brains lay splattered all over the walls?" Helen held everyone's attention. Then all eyes switched to me.

I pulled my injured finger out of my mouth. Helen's description of Calvin's death and the taste of my own blood made me gag.

I inhaled a deep breath, looked around the room, and tried to think of the best way to answer her.

"Well, I wouldn't say that's exactly how it looked. Porkchop was the first to find poor Calvin." I bit into a brownie I'd snatched before I returned to the group. I hoped my answer satisfied Helen's curiosity.

"Poor Calvin? He got what he deserved," Patsy said, her head bent over her frame. Her straight hair fell forward and hid her face. Fingers clutched her hook so tightly her knuckles turned white.

Why did *she* dislike Calvin so much? "Patsy, did Calvin do something to you?" This marked the second time she'd mentioned her hatred for him. Anyone would think it was more than a mild dislike for the man. Did she hate him enough to kill him? And for what reason?

Patsy glared at me from across the table and snapped, "I don't want to talk about it. Not that my feelings toward that evil man are any of your business, either."

I turned to Candie and whispered, "Did I hit a sore subject with her?"

Candie shrugged her shoulders. "I don't know, but she is awfully touchy about Calvin."

I nodded then picked up my rug hook to pull some loops. Thoughts of Patsy's reaction to my question tumbled about my brain. What had changed in her life that could have involved Calvin?

"Do you think he'll be laid out at Wilson's Funeral Home? I hope so. They have a drive-up viewing window. I hear it's the latest thing in funerals. Are you and George going to put one in at your place?" All eyes turned to Helen.

I shrugged my shoulders. I had read the town's other funeral home had installed a drive-up viewing window on the side of their Victorian-style building. According to *Funeral Homes, Today*, an industry magazine The Do Drop Inn subscribed to, this was the latest trend in the funeral business. A curtain covered the window and remained closed until a mourner drove up. An electronic eye signaled music to begin playing and the curtain parted to reveal the deceased. A retractable drawer opened and held a guest book for the mourner to sign. I believed in progress, but I thought this took things too far. Would people soon expect fries to go with their visit?

"I don't think we'll add one any time soon." Even though George hated for our funeral home's competitor to one-up us in any way, I hoped he wasn't thinking of adding one to The Do Drop. As his partner, I would have to nix that idea. I reached for a strip of the blue wool I had picked up from Lucy Saturday morning. I wanted to focus on the rug's sky, not Calvin's murder.

Helen pushed a pair of bright orange framed glasses up the bridge of her pointed nose. "I read where a funeral parlor in Jersey put one in but needed to install bulletproof glass, because of all the gangsters they bury."

Marybeth Higgins, a nurse who works the night shift at the Wings Falls Hospital, frowned. "Why would they need bulletproof glass? The person is already dead."

Helen glared at Marybeth. She didn't like having her word questioned. "I don't know. I read it on the Internet." According to Helen, if she read something on the Internet it made that information the gospel truth.

I could have pinched Helen for her big mouth. Marybeth, who was a younger member in our group, in her thirties, but one of the quieter ones, didn't often contribute to our weekly gab sessions. Usually, she sat and hooked during our Monday morning gatherings and didn't add much to the conversations swirling about the room. With Helen's rebuke, Marybeth sunk back into her shell.

The rest of the morning passed quickly. I glanced at my watch and saw it read noon. I began to pack up. I needed to stop at the police station before I headed home. Porchop would prance back and forth by my front door, waiting for his lunchtime kibbles.

"Leaving already?" Patsy asked. She had gotten over her earlier snit when I had questioned her about Calvin, but she'd remained unusually quiet today, as if something weighed on her mind.

"Yes, I have some errands to run before I go home. Porchop will be waiting by the front door for his food." I slid my hooking frame into my red tote bag.

"Tell Porchop Hana says hi."

I grinned. Patsy, like most dog owners, thought their pets acted human. "I will. How old is Hana now?"

Patsy smiled. "Going on six come November."

I next tucked my rug into the bag. "Was it only yesterday he was a pup? I remember him as a small ball of fur. You got him from Calvin's shelter, didn't you?"

Patsy's olive skin paled. She slid back her chair and stood. "Excuse me, I need to go to the ladies' room."

She scurried out of the room. What had I said to upset her? The only connection of her with Calvin that I could come up with was her dog, Hana. Was there something about Hana that she would kill Calvin over?

I waved goodbye to the remaining ladies and left to keep my appointment with Detective Johnson.

* * *

Fifteen minutes later, I swung my Bug into the parking lot of the Wings Falls Police Station. I parked next to a black and white police cruiser and rubbed my sweaty palms on the legs of my blue jeans and opened the car door. I stepped out of my car and looked at the square brick building. Why did police stations make me feel as if I had committed a crime? It's not like I did anything wrong. In fact, I came here to do my civic duty. I climbed the cement steps that led to the front door, then pulled open the heavy metal door. Phones rang in the background. I walked up to the counter. It separated the general public from the rest of the station. Behind a thick glass window sat a civilian employee. Wanda Thurston, according to the name tag pinned to her floral blouse. She greeted me with a wide smile, her white teeth providing a sharp contrast to her dark skin.

"Can I help you?" she asked. Her voice carried over a loudspeaker into the waiting room.

I spoke into a hole cut in the glass wall. "I'm here to talk to Detective Johnson. I believe he's expecting me." Butterflies danced the mambo in my stomach.

Wanda punched a few buttons on the console in front of her and talked into the headpiece nestled amongst her black wavy hair and wrapped around to her mouth.

"He'll be out in a minute. You can take a seat over there if you'd like." She pointed to a row of metal framed, padded chairs that lined the wall opposite the counter.

I thanked her and did as she said. My gaze wandered about the room while I waited for Detective Johnson. Dull brown paneling covered the walls. On the wall to my right hung a seal of the state of New York and pictures of the governor and the station chief. A large American flag hung from a pole in the corner. Brown and tan industrial tile covered the floor. Talk about utilitarian. Bright yellow and aquamarine might be a tad out of place here, but a nice pale taupe for the walls and the trim painted white would brighten things up somewhat.

"Ms. Davies, I'm glad you could stop by. I'm curious as to what you have to say."

My head jerked up. I hadn't heard Detective Johnson approach. Suddenly, my mouth became dry. Why did I wish I had dressed in something nicer than my jeans and blue striped jersey shirt? He'd replaced his denim shirt and jeans of yesterday with a maroon striped shirt, khaki pants, and navy blazer. My mouth curved into a wide smile when I noticed his tie emblazoned with SpongeBob SquarePants flipping Krabby Patties. I couldn't help the laugh that escaped my lips. I pointed to his tie. "A SpongeBob fan?"

"A weakness of mine, weird and goofy ties. Kind of a stress reliever. Whenever things get too tense, I only have to look at my tie. The guys razz me about them, but I can take it." He gestured to the metal door. "After you."

I snatched up my handbag I had placed on the floor next to my chair and stood.

He tapped on the glass window to get Wanda's attention. She nodded and pushed a button that released the lock on the door.

We walked into a large room. Uniformed and non-uniformed officers sat behind a mixture of scarred wooden and metal desks. While cell phones might rule the public, chunky black land-line phones sat on each desk along with laptops, piles of papers, photos of kids, and coffee mugs. The buzz in the room was deafening. A few of the officers waved as we walked past. Detective Johnson returned their greetings with a nod or a wave of his own. He ushered me into a private office.

"Please, take a seat." He pointed to a chair identical to the ones in the lobby. He sat behind a battered desk like the ones in the room we'd passed through. A wilting fern held court on the bookcase behind the desk. Another picture of the governor hung on the wall above it. Either the state had a surplus of these pictures, or the governor didn't want anyone to forget who ran the state. Florescent lights hung from the ceiling and cast an eerie glow on the same dull paneling covering the walls as in the reception area of the station. Brown tile lay underfoot. Geez, an interior designer I am not, but even I could have created a better atmosphere to work in.

"So, what do you want to add to your statement?"

He didn't waste any time getting to the heart of the matter. I cleared my throat. "Um, I forgot to mention, when I got out of my car at the shelter, I heard what sounded like wheels of a car speeding out of the back parking lot." I twisted my fingers together. Why did I think my statement condemned someone to death? I only wanted to report what I knew of Saturday morning to help solve Calvin's murder.

Detective Johnson leaned back in his chair. He twirled a pen between two fingers. "Did you notice the car or who drove it?"

"No, I only heard what sounded like wheels spinning on gravel. You know, when someone accelerates too fast and the wheels can't get traction." I held the handle to my purse in a death grip. Even though the air conditioning hummed in his office, sweat gathered between my shoulder blades.

He jotted this information on a piece of paper. "I will add this to your statement. Anything else?" he asked. He tapped his pen on his desktop.

I wanted to smooth back the lock of brown hair falling over his forehead.

"No, I've told you everything. I know it isn't much, but I knew I should tell you." I gathered up my purse and started to stand.

He leaned forward and placed his elbows on his paper-strewn desk. "You've been most helpful. What you told me helps with an anonymous tip someone phoned in."

My purse dropped to the tiled floor. My eyes shot to his. "Have you found the murderer?"

Detective Johnson placed his hands behind his head and leaned back in his chair. "Let's say we have some solid leads."

CHAPTER EIGHT

———

The Duprees serenaded me as I turned the Bug into my driveway. I parked in front of the garage door, turned off the ignition and closed my eyes. My head rested on the steering wheel. I needed a few minutes of calm before facing an energetic Porkchop, doing leaps and twirls as soon as I opened the front door. My meeting with Detective Johnson had left me frazzled. What unnerved me so much about him? I curled my fingers around the steering wheel to calm their shaking. True, I don't usually hang out in the Wings Falls Police Station, but I'd known Sergeant Joe Peters since kindergarten, so it wasn't like I'd never been around police before. Maybe it's because I'm a wee bit involved with Calvin Perkins' murder, but I would have to deal with that later. I didn't have any more time to waste on my crazy feelings. My dog awaited.

I and leaned over the passenger seat for my rug hooking tote, then walked up to my front door and noticed the mums needed a dose of water. A gardener I am not. If a plant survives in my yard, it's because it was determined to live and not my tender care. Porkchop's barks echoed behind the door. I pushed it open and was greeted by him jumping and leaping in the air. He could enter the doggie Olympic event for the high jump and win the gold medal hands down.

I dropped my hooking bag on the floor and reached down to pat his head. "Have you been a good boy while I was away?" He barked. I interpreted it to mean in doggie speak "You bet. Now give me something to eat. You are late and I have waited long enough."

"You are right, I am late. I stopped at the police station to talk to Detective Johnson." Porkchop cocked his head to the side and stared up at me. His ears twitched forward. I often thought he understood every word I said. His tail thumped the hardwood floor in my small entryway. A small growl rumbled out of his throat.

I patted his head again. "I know, you had to give him the tasty bone you chewed on, but it was kind of nasty. He thought it might be the murder weapon. You wouldn't want to impede the investigation."

Porkchop stood and ran into the kitchen. He'd had enough of my explanation, so I trailed along behind him. He jumped at the counter where his kibbles jar sat. I picked up his bone-shaped food bowl from the floor and scooped in a handful of his food. The kibbles clinked against the side of his bowl.

My stomach complained to my backbone, too. I opened the refrigerator door and peered inside. I needed to stop at the food store. My fridge offered slim pickings—a bagel, a tub of artificial butter and some dried-up cheese. I cut the crusty corners off the cheese and settled for grilled cheese on a bagel and a mug of tea. I filled the mug with water, placed a decaf tea bag in it and shoved it in the microwave to brew. I know, if I had any English ancestors, they'd be rolling in their graves right now at my tea-brewing technique, but quick sometimes won over quality. Two minutes later the microwave dinged. I took my mug and cheesy bagel and sat at the kitchen table to savor my meager fare. I was about to bite into my bagel when a loud banging on my front door echoed into the kitchen. The unmistakable voice of Gladys O'Malley shouted from the other side. "Sam, Sam, open up. Please, you have to help me."

I rose from my chair and placed my bagel on the counter so my future Olympic champion couldn't snatch it.

My sobbing neighbor collapsed into my arms as soon as the door opened.

I led the weeping Gladys over to my overstuffed sofa. "Gladys, what is the matter?"

She settled her thin body onto my sofa and dabbed at her eyes with a sodden handkerchief. Her helmet of orange-dyed curls channeled Albert Einstein.

Watery blue eyes looked up at me. "They've hauled Frank down to the police station. They're grilling him about Calvin's murder. Please. You discovered the body. You have to help prove my Pookie Bear's innocence."

I sat next to her and took one of her gnarled hands into mine. Pookie Bear, now that was a first. I will never look at

Frank Gilbert the same way again. "Gladys, when did this happen?"

"I got a call from him a few minutes ago. Do you know if they let the prisoner have only one phone call? Ohhh, a prisoner. My Pookie Bear locked up with all those hardened criminals. Will he have to get prison tattoos?" Gladys wailed.

I patted her hand. "Not if he doesn't want to. Anyway, I bet they only want to ask him a few questions." Gladys leaned a wee bit towards the dramatic. "What exactly did he say?"

Gladys hiccupped. "The police stopped by the animal hospital and said they wanted to talk to him about Calvin's murder. Apparently, a witness saw him leaving the shelter Saturday morning and someone confirmed this." Gladys's scrawny chest heaved in a shuddering breath.

I gulped. Had I put the proverbial nail in his coffin? "Why was he there?"

Gladys waved her soggy handkerchief in the air. "Oh, I don't know. Some silly thing about giving Calvin money. You know Frank, he's such a sweetheart. He loves animals so much. That's why when he isn't working at the animal hospital, he volunteers at the shelter. I bet he donated money to help with the upkeep of the shelter. Calvin always needed cash to keep it afloat."

I had to agree. It cost a huge amount of money to operate For Pet's Sake. Even though Calvin had personal issues, he ran a clean and safe shelter for needy animals.

"Please, Sam, you have to help Frank. I do not know who else to ask. You are always researching something. You dig up facts for those articles you write all the time. I know you can figure out who murdered Calvin."

I shifted in my seat. What could I say? I already had a ton of questions about Calvin's murder. Maybe by helping Frank I could keep Joe from pointing his stubby finger at me.

Gladys pinned me with her eyes. Tears ran down her weathered face. "I cannot ask Junior for help."

I shook my head. "Junior?" I asked.

"Oh, he's my nephew and new on the force. His mother, my sister Matilda, would skin me alive if I asked him. Remember, I mentioned him coming to dinner the other day and if you wanted to join us?"

Right, she did speak of it when we were at The Ewe.
The local newspaper, the *Tribune,* had mentioned that the
Wings Falls police department had hired a few new recruits, not
only Hank Johnson.

"Please Sam, will you help Frank?" Gladys squeezed
my hand. She had a vice-like grip for such a frail-looking lady.

What did I know about solving murders? My research
on the life cycle of a dragonfly for a magazine article didn't
qualify me as a crime buster. Guilt washed over me, though.
What if the information I gave Detective Johnson led to Frank's
possible arrest? But I could clear my name. Was that so awful of
me?

"Okay, I will give it a shot." Did I agree to Gladys's
request?

Gladys's wrinkled face beamed as she patted my hand.
"I knew I could count on you."

"I cannot promise anything." I was less and less sure of
myself.

"You will have my Frank home with me in no time."
Gladys stood and walked to the door. "I feel so much better. I
know you'll have my Pookie Bear home real soon and cuddling
with me."

After Gladys left Porkchop walked into the living room
and leapt onto the sofa.

He stared up at me with his chocolate brown eyes.
"What?" I asked.

"I know, I know I'm an idiot. I couldn't even tell when
my ex did the horizontal mambo with his secretary, and I think I
can solve a murder?"

I bent over and scratched between his ears. "What have
I gotten myself into? Who do I think I am, Nancy Drew? If I'm
going to get myself into deep doo-doo, I'm not crime-busting
alone." I reached into the back pocket of my jeans, pulled out
my cell phone, flipped it open, and punched in Candie's number.

*   *   *

Candie pushed a strand of wind-blown hair off her face.
"So, what's the plan? Why the shelter?" she asked.

She'd arrived at my house ten minutes after I'd called,
and I explained about Gladys's plea for me to help prove Frank

innocent. We sat at a red light on Glen Street in Candie's baby blue '73 Mustang convertible she'd named Precious. The top was down, and a warm breeze wrapped around us.

Since this was Monday, traffic was light. Most of the summer tourists had gone home until next weekend when down-staters, Jerseyites, and revelers from surrounding states would pack all roads leading to Lake George. I had some serious thinking to do before we arrived at Calvin Perkins' animal shelter. Mainly because I had no plan.

I closed my eyes and leaned back on the car's white leather seats. My mind whirled. Maybe the breeze would straighten out my jumbled thoughts, so I would know what to do next.

I sat up straight. "I have to start narrowing down suspects."

Candie stared at me. "Suspects? As in more than one?"

I nodded.

The light turned green, and the car behind us honked. "Down-stater," Candie grumbled. She turned her attention back to the road. It was a well-known fact that locals rarely, if ever, used their car horn. A person could sit at a traffic light and let it turn red before a local would lay on their horn. When a car beeped, area folk assumed it to be an impatient so-and-so from out of the area.

I turned in my seat to face her. "I can think of at least four people who disliked Calvin and maybe wanted him dead."

"Four?" Candie asked. She raised an eyebrow at my bold statement.

I held up my right hand. "One"—I lifted a finger—"Frank Gilbert. He and Calvin were involved in some type of 'deal' with Jacob." Up went another finger. "Two—Patsy Ikeda. Hana, her dog, was Patsy's connection with Calvin. He supposedly made it possible for her to adopt Hana. Three—Jacob Sorenson. Maybe Calvin was still angry about whatever Las Vegas proposition Jacob had roped him into and they had an argument that led to Jacob killing him." A fourth finger shot up. "And let's not forget the person who is usually the best suspect."

Candie looked at me. "Who would it be?"

"Candie!" I clutched the dashboard in front of me. We narrowly missed side-swiping a Mercedes. *Sorry,* I mouthed to the guy behind the wheel giving us the finger.

"Oops, my bad." Candie refocused her attention back on the road.

When my stomach released its grip from my throat, I waggled finger number four at her. "The spouse or significant other of the murder victim usually tops the person of interest list. You and she hinted that all was not Happy Valley between the two of them. So, I'd say number four would be Shirley."

Candie shook her head. "Shirley? I don't think so. She's got a kind heart and wouldn't hurt anyone."

Now why was my cousin so opposed to Shirley being a possible suspect?

CHAPTER NINE

―――――

"I still don't think Shirley could be a suspect." Candie turned her Mustang into the For Pet's Sake parking lot. The car's tires crunched on the gravel.

I pushed hair out of my eyes and stared at Candie. I loved riding in a convertible with the top down, but the end result was—hair looking like it lost a fight with an electric mixer. We parked in front of the shelter. Yellow crime scene tape dangled from the door handle.

"There's a light on." I pointed to the glow shining through the door's window. "Someone is in there. I hope it's Shirley—she's my prime suspect."

Candie pulled the key out of the ignition and stuffed it into her purse. Her eyes bore into mine. "Be careful what you say. Shirley had her reasons for not acting overly upset with Calvin's passing."

My curiosity got the best of me, a big fault of mine, along with my love of designer handbags. "So, you are saying she could have killed Calvin. I knew it, I knew it." I bounced in my seat. My hand shook with excitement as it hovered over the door handle. Now I needed to figure out a way to prove Shirley murdered Calvin so Gladys's Pookie Bear could warm her feet again sooner than later and I could breathe a sigh of relief. I didn't believe for one minute that Detective Johnson would arrest Frank. Fingers crossed, I hoped the police only wanted to ask him some questions.

Candie laid her soft, white hand on my arm. The sun winked off the jewels studding the rings on her fingers. If the Wings Falls Airport's landing lights ever failed, they'd only have to line the runway with her rocks. They sparkled enough to land a jumbo jet. "I'm not saying that at all, so don't judge Shirley too harshly."

I could sense Shirley's guilt right down to my toes. She killed Calvin. Slammed him in the head with the huge doggie bone, and now she wanted Frank Gilbert to take the fall.

Candie grabbed her purse and flounced out of the car mumbling.

Great, now I had ticked her off. I'd have to do some fast-talking and probably a trip to Martha's, the local ice cream parlor, for a hot fudge sundae, to smooth things over.

I flung my door open. "What did you say?" I dared to ask.

"If you must know, I said Calvin crawled lower than a snake's belly in a wagon rut." Candie huffed to the shelter's door, her sandals slapping the ground with each angry step.

"Why do you say that?" I grabbed my navy Ralph Lauren shoulder bag. I had changed from my black leather MK. I needed the extra boost Ralph gave my ego. How can a freelance writer afford such an expensive accessory? Well, there is always eBay, and sometimes I score big, but that was my little secret.

My peeved cousin turned as I caught up to her. "It is for Shirley to say, not me." Candie snapped her lips shut.

The reception area looked deserted. The din of barking dogs in the kennels at the back of the shelter filled the room. Shirley was probably tending to the animals since she would be in charge of the shelter because of Calvin's death. I pointed behind the desk. "There is where Calvin met with foul play." The bone Porkchop had claimed as his own no longer sat on the floor. I assumed it was at the police station in the evidence locker. The spilled kibbles bags sat neatly stacked against the cinder-block wall.

"Ewww." Candie's face paled whiter than Memaw Parker's sheets flapping on the line on a Monday morning.

"Here, sit." I pushed her onto one of the metal chairs lining the reception area's walls. "Put your head between your knees. I don't need you fainting."

"You're used to working with dead people. I don't want to even look down from the Pearly Gates and observe myself laid out in all my fabulous glory when I go to the Great Beyond," Candie mumbled from the folds of her skirt.

"There isn't even a dead person here. I only showed you where Calvin lay sprawled out on the floor. Besides, I didn't have anything to do with the bodies. George handled the dead person part of our business. I took care of the books. That was before he hired Anna and they began engaging in some late-night bump fuzzies." While I was still a partner in the business, I was no longer involved in the day-to-day operation.

Candie sat up and pushed hair out of her eyes. "Samantha, let it go. How many times do I have to tell you? You are better off without him?"

I nodded. "You're right. It's not like I'm still in love with him. Believe me I'm not. But it ties a knot in my pride knowing he cheated on me, and with her. I have rocks in my backyard with more brains than her."

Candie laughed. Auburn curls bounced about her head.

"Who's there? Unless you're here to adopt, I've closed the shelter until further notice. I cannot take on any more strays," a voice called from down the hallway leading off the reception area. A moment later, Shirley stood in the doorway

"Hi Candie," she said walking towards us. Shirley frowned when she saw me. "Oh, and it's you."

Plan, I needed a plan. Why were we here? "I've come to apologize about what I said at Sweetie Pie's yesterday." Candie looked at me with a puzzled look in her eyes. I shrugged my shoulders. What can I say? I'm a quick, okay sometimes reckless, thinker.

"Um, yes she's sorry for acting so insensitive," Candie said. I tugged on the sleeve of her gauzy peasant blouse. Enough already, I wasn't that heartless.

Dirt streaked the front of Shirley's white T-shirt. She rubbed her large hands down the legs of her jeans. Hair escaped her braid and hung about her face. "Yeah, well, all right. Apology accepted."

She slumped into the chair Candie had vacated. "I'm a little overwhelmed right now. I helped Calvin with the animals. Fed them and cleaned their cages, you know. Me and our volunteers. But the police don't want anyone in here until tomorrow, so I had to call my help and say not to come in today. That new guy from Albany, he got a search warrant for the place, but Calvin's office is such a mess I don't know if they found anything. For now, it leaves everything up to me. I was in his office trying to go through some of his papers to find out if he left an insurance policy. I don't know how I am going to pay for the idiot's funeral."

I cocked an eyebrow at Candie. I wanted to shout, "I told you so. She isn't about to pull out her black mourning dress."

Shirley sucked in a breath. By the startled look on her face, she realized what she had said. "I know it sounds harsh, and you probably think I killed him, but I didn't, much as I would have loved to when he drank and used me as a punching bag."

I gasped. I never would have thought that as strong as Shirley looked, she would put up with such treatment from Calvin or any other man. Her arms had muscles riding piggyback.

She must have noticed the shocked look on my face. "Didn't Candie tell you? You two are so close and all. I thought for sure she would have told you about Calvin and me and why I went to the Women's Center." She looked from me to Candie. I shook my head.

Candie walked over to Shirley, bent down, and hugged her. "What you told me there remains confidential. I would never breathe a word to anyone."

I had to ask, "Why did you stay with him?"

Tears pooled in her eyes. "After he sobered up, he'd act so sorry and beg me to forgive him."

I gritted my teeth. What George did was bad enough, but if he'd ever raised a hand to me, Lorena Bobbitt would have looked like Mother Teresa when I got done with him.

Shirley's shoulders trembled as sobs shook her body. "I don't know what to do or where to begin. The office is such a mess."

"Look, I did this kind of work at the funeral parlor, taking care of the books, filing papers. Maybe I can help you straighten things out." Candie looked at me as if I had grown another head.

A shaky smile spread across Shirley's face. "If you're sure. I guess you can tell by all the barking it is feeding time and I need to tend to the critters."

"I'm sure." I stuffed my hands into the pockets of my jeans to stop myself from rubbing them together with glee. What an open invitation to poke into Calvin's business.

"You'll find the office down the hall, second door on the right." She wiped the tears from her eyes and pointed towards the hall. "I need to get back to the animals. From all the racket, they're getting impatient."

"Have you lost your marbles? What are you up to?" Candie hissed at me as we walked down the hall.

"Look, someone hated Calvin bad enough to kill him. There may be clues in his office. And I wouldn't rule out Shirley, yet. Maybe he hit her one time too many."

Candie shook her head at me. "Puleeease. Couldn't you tell how upset she got when she thought we'd think she'd killed Calvin?"

Before I pushed the scarred wooden door open, I turned to her. "You said she performed as a professional wrestler, right?"

"Yes, that's what she told me. Shirley the Slammer. She said she did rather well, too. Even won a championship."

"A big part of wrestling is about showmanship." I turned the doorknob to Calvin's office.

Candie frowned. "Huh?"

I pointed towards the reception area. "Acting. Out there, in the reception area, could have been all an act."

"Ugh!" My shoulders drooped in dismay when I opened the door. Unlike the reception area, Calvin's office looked like a train wreck. Papers covered the desktop, along with crumpled bags from fast-food restaurants. McDonalds must have been his favorite. Paper coffee cups littered the floor near the trash can. Obviously, he didn't care or have good aim. File cabinet drawers gaped open and manila folders spilled out. A pinup calendar hung over his desk. Miss August heated up the page wearing little more than her sunny smile.

Candie slumped against the door. "Good night a livin'. Where do we even start? Do you think the police found anything in this mess? And what are we looking for?"

I shook my head. It'd be easier to teach Porkchop to sing "Jailhouse Rock" than find clues in this mess. I'd need a ton of luck and a bushel of prayers to keep the police from carting Frank off to the Big House. "I don't know, anything to give us an idea as to why someone would murder Calvin."

I kicked paper cups out of my way and walked towards the desk. "I will take the desk. You start with the file cabinet."

Candie pushed herself off the door and saluted. "Yes, ma'am."

I stuck my tongue out at her then began to pull out desk drawers.

"Holy french fry!" Candie screeched.

I jumped. "What, what? Did you find something already?"

"Yeah, a french fry stuck to the bottom of my sandal." Candie held up her shoe for my inspection.

I struggled to contain my giggles, afraid she would launch the offending fry at me.

* * *

"I'm done in," Candie said from the middle of the floor. File folders covered her lap, their contents strewn on the floor around her.

We'd looked for over two hours for a clue I hoped would scream, "I killed Calvin Perkins." Shirley poked her head in a few times, but I assured her we had things under control. Right, as under control as me at a designer handbag sale.

"I have to agree. I don't know what I'm going to tell Gladys." Her Pookie Bear might have to pick out his prison tattoos sooner than later. And I wasn't any closer to erasing myself from Joe Peters' suspect list either.

My body had become stiff from sitting hunched over the desk. I rolled my shoulders. Stretching my neck back, I stared at the dusty ceiling. My eyes widened. What was that on the ceiling tile over the desk—smudges?

"What's that?" I pointed to the ceiling

Candie crawled over to me. The folders she had been sorting spilled off her lap. "What? Did you find something?"

"Here, hold this chair so it doesn't slip out from under me."

Candie stood and grabbed on to the back of the chair. I held on to her shoulder and climbed onto its seat.

"Be careful. You could fall and break a bone. What would Detective Johnson say, then?"

I kicked papers and trash out of my way and got onto the desktop. I didn't even want to think about that conversation. If he even cared enough if I injured myself.

I pointed to a ceiling tile. "Up there. Those are smudge marks on this tile."

Candie nodded.

I lifted the tile and a small, wrapped package fell out onto the desktop skimming my shoulder.

I frowned. "Why would Calvin place something up there? It isn't an accessible place."

"Only if he had something to hide," we both said at the same time then high-fived each other.

With Candie's help I got off the desk. At least I hadn't sustained any injuries to report to Hank. I scrounged in the desk drawer for something to rip off the tape wrapped around the package. I pushed aside a stapler, paper clips and stickie notes until my hands clamped around a pair of scissors.

"Here give them to me." Candie grabbed the scissors out of my hands and cut the tape.

"Be careful," I said.

A black book, small enough to cradle in the palm of my hand, emerged from the wrapping.

Candie peered over my shoulder. I opened the tattered book to the first grease-stained page. Calvin must have chomped on a Big Mac when writing. We both gasped at what he had scrawled in his little Black Book.

CHAPTER TEN

"What does all this mean?" Candie and I flipped through the dog-eared and stained pages of the book for at least five minutes. Bizarre entries filled the tattered pages, Calvin's handwriting little more than a scribble. Some dated as far back as five years.

"Beats me." Candie frowned. "Why would he buy one hundred and fifty dollars of pacifiers and one hundred dollars' worth of jump ropes. He must have had one whopping headache if he spent one hundred dollars on aspirin every month."

I thumbed through the pages of the Black Book. "Hmmm."

$100 —peanuts
$100 —aspirin
$100—jump ropes
$100—lotto tickets
$150—pacifiers

"This looks like a strange list, but the entries don't all start at the same time." I pointed to a smudged page. The pacifiers weren't listed on the first pages of the book. Nor the peanuts.

Now I frowned and tapped the page. "Look at this page he labeled *Peanuts*. He scribbled dates below the word a whole year after the ones headed *Aspirin, Jump ropes*, and *Lotto tickets*. That would make it four years ago. Do you think he had a sudden yen for peanuts?" I looked at my cousin's equally puzzled face.

She shook her head. "Darned if I know. And it's a pretty good lottery habit if he spent one hundred dollars a month on them. Look, he didn't start buying pacifiers until about six months ago. Why would he need so many? Shirley never said she and Calvin expected a baby. This has to have some sort of meaning other than Calvin's weird spending habit."

"You're right. She'd have to give birth to octuplets to need so many, and she'd still have a few left over." I turned to the last entry written in the book. "Now why would the price of a baby's binkie go up to a hundred and fifty dollars?"

Candie shook her head. "Beats me. One mean mystery surrounded Calvin. He should have hired a cleaning staff and a fumigator for his office, instead of spending his money on all this other foolishness." She waved her ringed hand in front of her nose.

I nodded. "You are right. The greasy smell from his leftover fries and hamburger wrappers would make a warthog gag."

Candie ran a hand through her hair. "I will have to take at least two bubble baths and stir in some of my extra lavender-infused crystals when I get home to get the smell off me. I have a date with Mark tonight. He will think I had dunked myself in a vat of chicken grease if I don't."

A smile spread across her face. The dreamy look in her eyes told me that she no longer sat in the trash heap of Calvin's office, but anticipated her evening with Mark.

I snapped my fingers in front of Candie's face. "Earth to Candie."

She blinked, then sighed. "So, what do you think all this means?" She pointed at the book I clutched in my hand.

"I haven't any idea. Maybe he had some weird spending habits. Or." My head shot up. "Do you think he wrote this in some kind of code?"

"Code? What would he need to use code words for?" Candie asked.

Our eyes snapped to each other. "Blackmail," we said at once.

I put a finger to my lips. "Shh."

"How are things going back here?" asked an unexpected voice. "Any luck finding an insurance policy or anything that will pay for putting Calvin six feet under?"

My cousin and I jumped. We were unaware Shirley had entered the office. I shoved the Black Book into a crumbled Big

Mac takeout bag that vied for space on the desk with empty soda cans.

"Ah, we're still looking. You have a bigger mess on your hands than any of us can handle. You might want to hire a cleaning crew. We'll put any important files we find in the cabinet, but I think the rest of this amounts to trash." I waved my fingers at the litter spread across the desk and floor.

"A cleaning crew? Aren't they expensive? I don't know if I can afford to plant Calvin in the ground let alone hire someone to clean up this mess." Shirley shook her head, despair etched on her face. "I never knew it looked like such a disaster in here. Calvin always kept the door locked. He didn't allow anyone in here. I only got the key to this room this morning. Detective Johnson came by and returned it to me. Apparently, Calvin had his key ring in his pocket. Detective Johnson didn't think the keys were necessary for the case anymore since they had finished searching the place. I thought that was real nice of him."

I cocked an eyebrow at Candie. "Let me send over the people we use at the funeral parlor. The owner of Clean Sweep owes me a favor anyway. I gave him a discount on a casket for his grandma. One was delivered to the funeral parlor with a few scratches, but nobody noticed them once we had draped the casket with a cloth and surrounded it with flowers."

Shirley dug a torn tissue out of her jeans pocket and blew her nose. "Thanks so much. I would appreciate it." She looked about the litter-strewn room and shook her head. "You'd never guess by the look of this mess we keep the shelter so spotless."

I nodded in agreement. Dachshund-shaped earrings slapped against my neck. Every Christmas, my mother gave me dachshund-themed presents. One year it was a pair of socks emblazoned with my favorite fur buddies. Another year she gave me a dachshund-shaped change purse. I love my parents with all my heart, but enough already. But since I am such a dutiful daughter, I could never break their hearts and tell them such a thing. So, I would always smile and gush over the presents. "Looks like he led a double life, doesn't it? And he obviously loved fast food joints from all the paper bags and wrappers tossed about." I nudged one with my toe. "Did he ever have a craving for peanuts?"

"Peanuts?" Shirley wrinkled her brow. "No, he was allergic to them. He broke out in hives if he ate only one. Why do you ask?"

I stumbled for an answer. My mind went blank.

Thank heavens, Candie acted quicker on her feet with an answer and came to my rescue. "Ahh, my mistake. I mentioned to Sam I thought I saw him coming out of the Nut House the other day. You know, the new gourmet snack store on Glen Street."

"It must have been someone else. When I first started to live with him, I brought a can of peanut brittle home. I love the stuff. Well, I thought he was going to burst a blood vessel when I offered him some. He grabbed the can out of my hand and threw it in the trash. Told me never to bring any kind of peanut into the house again. Not if I didn't want to be tossed out, too. But I guess you can tell he wasn't allergic to fast food." Shirley waved her hand in the direction of Calvin's desk.

She looked at me. Tears swam in her eyes. "I appreciate your offer." She gave us a weak laugh. "You wouldn't happen to have any more of them scratch and dent coffins at the funeral parlor, would you?"

"I will talk to George and find out what he can do. Would you mind if I take this home for Porkchop?" I pointed at the McDonald's bag I had shoved the Black Book into. "I guess Calvin didn't finish all of his Big Mac, and Porkchop would think he got a big treat." I would never give Porkchop something not fresh off the grill, but Shirley did not have to know it, and I also imagined she was too overwhelmed to notice.

Shirley waved a hand at the bag. "Sure, sure. Take whatever you want. It's one less thing I have to trash."

"You ready to hit the road, Candie? I know you've got a big date tonight." I nodded to her and grabbed the McDonald's bag off the desk.

She patted her hair. "Oh, yeah. Got to get home and get myself fancied up."

I stopped in the doorway and turned back to Shirley. "One last thing, were you and Calvin expecting?"

Shirley blanched. She swayed and grabbed the edge of the desk "No. Why do you ask?"

"No reason. If you need any further help, give either me or Candie a call."

Candie turned the key in the ignition of her Mustang. The motor roared to life. She shifted into gear. "Where to now?" she asked. We pulled out of the parking lot of the shelter.

I shoved a strand of hair behind my ears. "You'd better drop me off at home. You'll need some time to get ready for your date with Mark, and I'm sure Porkchop has to be let out."

She slid her sunglasses up her nose. "As I said, I'm going to need some extra soaking and shampooing to get the stench of his office off my body. What did you mean by asking Shirley if she and Calvin expected a baby?"

"I'm trying to get some answers to this mystery. If she had become pregnant, maybe that's why Calvin bought pacifiers. But even if she was, I would think it's an awful lot of money to shell out for them." I may never have attained motherhood, but even I know for one hundred and fifty dollars a binkie had better be gold-plated.

My cousin regarded me. "Sam, you don't still think Shirley killed Calvin, do you?"

Traffic picked up as we headed towards downtown Wings Falls. I peeked at my watch. The hands pointed to a few minutes past three thirty. The restaurants lining Glen Street bustled with hungry diners.

"I have to admit, I have my doubts. Like I said, she could be acting. She mentioned Calvin used to beat on her. What if she couldn't take it any longer and slugged him with the bone? You know, in a fit of anger or maybe temporary insanity. The bone was big enough to do a great amount of damage. It was as large as Porkchop."

Wind whipped Candie's hair around her face. I opened my purse and dug inside for a rubber band. I pushed aside gum wrappers, pens, crumpled Walmart receipts. Finally, I found a black scrunchie.

I held it out to her. "Here, at the next red light pull your hair back before we have an accident."

She stuck her tongue out at me but did as I asked. "Hmmm, temporary insanity. I guess someone beating you could push anyone over the edge."

"Right, it's why I say she's still my main suspect. Look, look." I pointed a finger to a couple sitting at a table on the patio outside Momma Mia's.

My cousin swerved into the opposite lane. A car blared its horn at us. She narrowly missed the car. "Why don't you scare me to death?" she asked and exhaled a deep breath.

I nodded towards the restaurant. "Quick, look at who's eating together. An odd couple if you ask me." *Really odd indeed,* I thought.

CHAPTER ELEVEN

———

"What? Who?" Candie pulled the Mustang back into our lane. Car horns honked at our near bumper kissing.

I held my hand next to my face. "Don't stare."

"How am I supposed to see who's sharing a late lunch if I don't look?"

The traffic light turned red. "Okay, okay, but look natural. Act like you're adjusting the radio or something." I slid down in my seat so Candie could have a better look at the diners.

"Jeanine, the receptionist from the vet's office, and is that Jacob, her ex sitting next to her?" Candie's voice rose an octave.

I rolled my eyes and hissed at her. "Shh."

"But you said Jeanine couldn't stand him and that she didn't have two kind words to say when you asked about their past romance." She gave me a poke. "Don't you think it's odd they'd eat lunch together, although it doesn't exactly look like a friendly meal."

I ignored my own advice not to stare and sat up and glanced over at them. Sure enough, Jacob and Jeanine were in the midst of an argument. Jeanine was doing a good job throwing dagger-eyes at Jacob. If looks could kill, Jacob would soon join Calvin at The Do Drop Inn Funeral Parlor.

"Oops, I think their meal has ended," Candie said. She nodded in their direction.

It had. Jeanine stood and grabbed her purse from under the table.

Honk. So much for trying not to act obvious. The light had switched to green and the driver of the car behind us leaned on their horn. Jeanine and Jacob looked over and glared at Candie and me. I waggled my fingers in a faint wave.

"Down-stater," Candie mumbled under her breath as we pulled away from the light. "Why do you think they ate lunch together?"

I swiveled in my seat to face Candie. "Darned if I know, but I find it strange. By the way Jeanine gave Jacob the evil eyeball, I don't think they have rekindled their old romance."

"Too bad Mark and I didn't sit at the next table. I have extremely good hearing, you know. Maybe I could have eavesdropped on what they argued about."

"Why is one of our murder suspects trying to get so chummy with Jeanine? Your   doing a little listening in on their conversation would have come in handy." I tapped my fingers against my chin. "Maybe I will have to do a little more research on the article about how Doc Sorenson became a veterinarian. I will give Jeanine a call in the morning to set up an appointment." We pulled up to my house, and Candie swung the Mustang into my drive.

Candie's fingers drummed the steering wheel. Worry lines creased her forehead. "Sam, be careful. I think there is more to Jeanine and Jacob's relationship than she is letting on. You go scratching a hound in the wrong place, and you're likely to get bit."

"Don't you give it another thought. Go home and take a long soak and enjoy your night out with Mark. I will want blow by blow details in the morning." I pulled on the door handle and stepped out of the car.

Candie leaned across the front seat towards me. "Sam, why don't you ask that hunky detective out? What's his name? Joe, Pete, Brian…?"

I leaned against the car door with my mouth open. "It's Hank, and why would I ask him out? I barely know him."

Candie drummed her ruby-red fingernails on the dashboard in irritation. "Close your mouth or a bug might fly in. For one thing, you could stop living your love life through my dates with Mark. Second, you need more companionship than a dog, and last, but not least, he's new in town. What better excuse do you need to ask someone out than to make them welcome?"

I held up my fist and flicked up an index finger. I was getting pretty good at using my digits to prove my point. "First, I do not live my love life through your and Mark's dates. I only ask to make conversation. See if I ever ask again." Finger number two flipped up. "Porkchop is loyal and loving. He's the best companion I could ever want. He can keep my feet warm better than any man and with none of the hassle." A third finger joined the other two. "I will look up the number to the local Welcome Wagon and inform them I know someone new has moved into town."

I turned on my heels and marched up to my front door. Candie honked as she drove down the street. I gave her a backhanded wave, then pushed my key into the lock. The sound of Porkchop scratching on the other side drifted through the door. In my mind's eye, his long body shook back and forth as his tail wagged in warp speed.

"So, did you miss me, boy?" I asked as the door swung open. "How about a snack?" I bent and scratched Porkchop's back. As I had imagined, his tail wagged as fast as Superman's speeding bullet.

My dog followed me into the kitchen. His short legs scurried to keep up with me and his promised meal.

I scooped kibble into his doggie bowl then glanced at my answering machine. A red number two flashed on and off. I grabbed a mug out of a kitchen cabinet, filled it with water, and dropped in a teabag. With my mug in the microwave and the *Start* button pushed, I pulled a stool up to my kitchen counter to listen to the messages on my answering machine. The first call came from a telemarketer trying to sell me new siding for my house. Guess he didn't know my house was built of brick. So much for researching potential clients. I deleted the message and hit play once more.

"Ms. Davies, Bob Spellman here—associate editor at Rolling Brook Press. We're interested in your manuscript, *Porkchop, The Wonder Dog.* I'm sorry we didn't connect. The rest of my day and tomorrow morning are filled with meetings, so please call me after two tomorrow at 610-555-1212."

My mouth dropped open. I had submitted the manuscript featuring my Porkchop to Rolling Brook Press, over six months ago. What with all my freelance article writing, I'd pushed it to the back of my mind. Well, maybe not all the way back. I still had all my fingers and toes crossed in hopes of them publishing my book. I scooped Porkchop into my arms and we happy-danced around my small kitchen, knocking into a chair as we swirled past.

I held him at arm's length and looked in his eyes. "Can you believe it, a phone call, not even an email? This must be good news, right?" My pup cocked his head and stared back at me. "Okay, okay, so the only thing you're interested in is a romp outside and a full belly but think about it. This book could make you, and hopefully me, famous. Why there could even be *Porkchop, The Wonder Dog* merchandise. I could write a movie about your adventures. We'd make Snoopy look like a has-been."

Visions of mega-buck contracts and movie deals swam before my eyes. I even envisioned Porkchop's star on the Hollywood Walk of Fame.

The microwave's dinging signaled my tea had finished brewing and snapped me back to the present. The clock on the microwave read four o'clock. "Drat, I missed his phone call. It's probably too late to call him back tonight. No, I can't do that. He said to call him back tomorrow after two. I glanced down at my puppy who sat at my feet happily finishing off his kibble, oblivious to the butterflies bouncing around my stomach.

I rummaged around in a cupboard for the package of Pepperidge Farms dark chocolate chip cookies I had hid behind the flour canister to have with my tea. I figured out of sight out of mind, but the phone call from Bob Spellman needed celebrating. What better way than with some chocolate? I grabbed my tea and the bag of cookies plus a rawhide bone. Porkchop could celebrate, too. He followed me into the living room where we snuggled into the corner of my sofa. I set my tea and cookies on the end table and threw the bone on the floor for him to gnaw on. After I finished off half the bag of cookies and drained my mug dry, my eyes began to droop. It had been a long and exhausting day.

* * *

"Come on, you can jump higher. I said jump higher. Look at you, so out of shape. What kind of wimp are you?" I fell as a jump rope tangled around my ankles.

"Can't you hear those babies crying? Do something to make them stop. Put a binkie in their mouths." I covered my ears to drown out the deafening sound of crying babies. "Ouch!" An unseen figure pelted me with binkies.

"You are a loser. Nothing but a loser. You will never win no matter how long you play." Lotto tickets floated onto my lap.

"You said you had a headache. Here take one of these. Not enough, take more. Need some more? Here you go." A giant-size aspirin bottle walked towards me.

"You said you liked peanuts. Have some more and more and more." A hand shoved peanuts into my mouth. I gagged. A loudspeaker blared "Take Me Out to the Ball Game."

* * *

My eyes flew open, and my face was wet. Porkchop sat on my chest licking cookie crumbs off my face. The clock above my TV read seven. The sun peeked through the window next to my wing chair.

"Oh, my goodness. Porkchop, it's morning. I cannot believe I slept all night on the sofa. And the dreams I had, more like nightmares. Jump ropes and binkies attacked me. Wait a minute." I leapt off the sofa and ran to my den/office. I flipped open my laptop and powered it on. My fingers tapping the desktop showed my impatience. My screensaver flashed on a picture of Porkchop. Who else? I quickly connected to the internet. If my hunch proved right, I had a clue to a person in Calvin's Black Book and his possible murderer. I researched a few sites then I picked up the phone and dialed Candie's number.

"This had better be good. My eyes aren't even awake, yet." The voice on the line was hoarse and scratchy as it mumbled to me.

A smile crept across my face. I imagined a rumpled and sleepy Candie.

"Take me out to the ball game. Give me some peanuts and crackerjacks," I sang into the phone.

"Are you crazy? You have lost it, waking me up to your caterwauling. I think you've damaged my hearing. What time is it anyway? OMG, seven thirty! I've only been asleep for two hours. If you were here right now, I'd strangle you." My cousin clearly didn't appreciate my early morning call or my singing. So, I wasn't Beyonce.

"No, I haven't lost it, but I think I've figured out what or should I say who peanuts referred to in Calvin's Black Book. Be ready in thirty minutes. I will be by to pick you up. We are going to pay suspect number one a visit."

CHAPTER TWELVE

––––––––

"Promise me next time you have a bright idea, you will conjure it up at a more decent hour, not the middle of the night." Candie flipped open her compact mirror and swiped Passion Pink lipstick across her full lips.

"It is not the middle of the night. It's eight thirty in the morning. Most of Wings Falls woke up hours ago and is going about their business." To say my cousin Candie doesn't fall into the morning person column is like saying the Arctic gets a little cold. I flicked on the turn signal and headed my Bug down Main Street. "See I told you so. Sweetie Pie's is packed." I pointed to the customers lined up outside the restaurant. "Franny's been serving up her special Southern cooking for hours."

"I know I'm whining, but you interrupted a delicious dream about Mark drifting through my sleep." Candie clicked the compact mirror shut and shoved it and the tube of lipstick into her purse. She turned to face me. "How did you come to the conclusion peanuts meant Patsy, and what excuse did you give her for our visit?"

"Peanuts are a favorite at ballparks, and Patsy loves to play softball. I told her I wanted to interview her about Hana's breed. I scanned the Internet and discovered information about Japanese Spitz being a rare breed of dog." I had called Patsy right after my wake-up call to Candie. After I'd apologized to Patsy about the early hour, I gave her the excuse that a last-minute call from a dog magazine needed an article on Hana's breed ASAP.

Patsy lived in South Wings Falls, a part of town that saw major development after WWII when the soldiers returned home.

I turned down a tree-lined street and kept my eyes peeled for her house. Most of the homes were long, low ranch-style houses nestled behind decades-old shrubbery, probably planted by those returning soldiers. Hers, a ranch-style house from the post-war era, was constructed of white-washed brick.

"Keep an eye out for number seven. If I remember correctly, a Buddha statue sits next to her mailbox." I had visited Patsy's a few years ago when she hosted the Loopy Ladies' Christmas party.

"There, over there." Candie pointed down the street to a ranch. Her purse tumbled onto the floor of my car.

"Okay, okay." I turned the Bug into Patsy's drive and switched off the ignition. I sat there with my hands on the wheel and stared at the house.

"What are you waiting for? Patsy could be our killer," Candie said.

If I didn't know better, I'd think my cousin pictured herself as a modern-day Annie Oakley with a six-shooter hidden in her cavernous handbag. She chomped at the old bit to make a citizen's arrest.

"I don't have a plan. I mean we cannot tromp up the steps, knock on the door and when Patsy opens it say 'Nice day, Patsy. Oh, and by the way did you kill Calvin Perkins?'"

"Yeah, I guess you are right. Having a plan might be a good idea. How about if we…"

Candie detailed an idea from the latest romance novel/murder mystery she had outlined and was ready to start writing. She wanted to branch out in her writing and add a little murder to her plots along with the romance.

"I guess it's as good as any." I shook my head. It sure beat stuttering my way through an unplanned interrogation.

Patsy answered on my second knock. "Hi," I said and waved to her through the screen door. Barking echoed from inside the house. "I hope you don't mind, my cousin Candie joining us. She stopped by unexpectedly this morning and woke me at the crack of dawn." I masked a forced yawn with my hand.

"Ouch." I rubbed the arm Candie had pinched.

Patsy opened the door and ushered Candie and me into the living room. "No, you're fine. Hana and I were enjoying a cup of tea. I mean I drank the tea and Hana gobbled his morning kibble." Her broad face split into a grin.

Rice paper watercolor prints hung on the walls. A small smiling Buddha statue, like the one by her mailbox, sat on a black lacquered table in front of her sofa. A smile tugged at my lips as I spied what looked like a fifty-six-inch flat-screen TV. It hugged the wall across from the sofa. The East meets West I guess, but maybe not so much as the TV was probably manufactured overseas, too.

Hana bounded across the Persian rugs spread over the floor. I bent and ruffled his thick fur while he sniffed my leg.

I straightened and said, "He probably smells Porkchop."

"I imagine so. Have a seat." Patsy motioned us to the sofa. Hana lay at her feet, his head rested on his paws. "So, what do you want to know about Japanese Spitz? You said you need information for an article you're writing."

I fumbled in my black and white paisley print Vera Bradley handbag for a pad of paper and pen. Finally, I found what I was looking for. I flipped open the pad and with pen poised over it asked, "Umm yes. How long have you had Hana? Why did you pick his breed? Are they barky? He barked when we knocked on the door."

"My, my, you do have a lot of questions. My Hana is a pleasure. I guess you'd say he means everything to me. As you know, I didn't marry so he's become the child I never had." Patsy reached down and caressed Hana's small, furry white head.

I could relate to what Patsy said as Porkchop was my one true love. I couldn't picture life without him, especially after I discovered what a sleaze George turned out to be.

"Hana's breed is a happy dog and wonderful with children. And for the barky part, they consider themselves the protector of your house. Better than an alarm system. A firm voice will control the barking. Aren't I right, my Hana?" She stroked the fur on his back.

"Do you mind if I use your bathroom?" Candie asked, about to put our quickly devised plan in action. While I interviewed Patsy, she'd snoop. I told her how I remembered Patsy had a den/office from my previous visit. "I'm afraid my morning coffee is calling." Candie did a little wiggle in her seat to emphasize the urgency of her situation.

Patsy twisted on the sofa and pointed to the hall behind us, leading off the living room. "Of course, dear. The bathroom is down the hall, second door on your left."

Patsy turned back to me and asked, "Did you get everything I've told you?"

I blinked. I hadn't noticed my pen still hovered over the pad of paper sitting on my lap, the pages blank. I hadn't written anything down, yet. "Ahhh, sure, I have a great memory. You might say I have the memory of an elephant. I remember everything people tell me. Comes in handy."

"I guess it would in your line of work. Especially, if you forget your pen and paper." Patsy giggled at her own joke.

"Yes, it does," I said. I had to keep Patsy talking to give Candie enough time to snoop. My eyes scanned the room. Filmy curtains covered a bay window that looked out onto the street. An arched doorway framed the dining room off the living room. A row of trophies lined the shelf next to the large flat-screen TV across from the sofa we sat on.

I pointed towards the shelves. "Those trophies—did you win them? I was told you have an awesome softball pitch."

Pink colored her wrinkled cheeks. "Yes, my team from the Senior Center has beaten the pants off the neighboring senior teams five years in a row."

If I didn't know better, I'd say petite little Patsy grew three inches as she sat up straighter on the sofa. Pride beamed from her face while she talked about her softball team.

"I bet it requires a good deal of practice on your part."

Patsy looked at me quizzically.

"You know pitching all those, what do you call it, strikes?" Remember I was the school nerd, not the athlete. Sports were not my favorite subject, other than when I drooled over some of the good-looking jocks like the other hormone-surging teens in my high school. "You must have a good pitching arm."

She flexed her small but muscular arm at me. It looked to me like she could swing a mean animal bone if she became mad enough. "I have a pitching area set up in my basement. I need to practice every day if we want to nab the Upstate Senior Softball championship again next year. There's even talk about a statewide playoff, but the organizers are concerned the games may cause too much stress on some of the seniors. Don't want anyone to suffer a stroke or heart attack, you know."

I coughed and shook my head. "Right, you don't want to lose any of your team members."

Patsy threaded her fingers through Hana's fur then looked at me. "You know in Japan they consider the Japanese Spitz a national treasure."

"You've mentioned at Loopy Ladies that you are a first-generation Japanese American." I needed to draw out our conversation to give Candie more time.

Patsy's eyes clouded over. "Yes, in fact, I have an older brother and sister who were born in an internment camp in California during World War II."

I shook my head. "That was such a sad statement of the times."

Patsy's gray-streaked black hair skimmed her shoulders as she nodded. "Yes, it was, but there's no use holding a grudge. My parents raised me and my siblings to be proud Americans and equally proud of our heritage. Every few years, I fly back to Japan to visit relatives."

"Why is Hana's breed considered a national treasure?" I asked, wondering how much longer I could draw this conversation out without her becoming suspicious of Candie's absence.

"Well, for many years the authorities did not allow the dogs out of Japan. They wanted to keep all the dogs there. It became impossible to get one imported to the United States."

"So how did you adopt Hana? You've had him for, what, almost six years now?" By the way Patsy averted her eyes and squirmed in her seat I knew I had hit a nerve. "Did you get him on one of your trips back to Japan?"

Patsy's fingers twisted on her lap. "Oh, things have changed. People breed them in this country now. Say, is your cousin all right? She's been gone a while." She stood and peered down the hall. As if on cue, the toilet flushed, and the bathroom door opened.

"Excuse me, sorry I took so long. It might have been something I ate last night. I think I have a case of the, you know…" Candie put on her best Southern girl act. She wouldn't say the word diarrhea, or even worse, the runs. She even managed to blush. I raised the pad of paper to my mouth to hide my smile.

"I guess we should get going then." I opened my purse and shoved in my pen and paper. "Candie, your cell phone takes pictures, right. Let's snap a picture of Patsy and Hana together."

Patsy gasped and a look of panic flashed across her face. "Ummm, I don't think it would be a good idea."

Patsy must have noticed the confusion on my face.

"He's camera shy," Patsy said as she bent down and cradled Hana's head in her arms. "Would a picture of only me be okay?"

Candie took the picture. I promised Patsy a copy of the magazine when it came out then thanked her for her time as we left.

On the drive back to my house I said, "Don't you find it strange what she said about Hana? What dog is camera shy? And she is so proud of Hana, so why wouldn't she want him featured in a national magazine? And your timing. We barely got out of there without being caught. You had me sweating big time. Patsy asked what happened to you right when you opened the bathroom door. And your excuse, great thinking, but did you find anything?"

"Pull over. I cannot wait to get to your house to show you my discovery."

I turned into the parking lot of a small strip mall. "What, what?"

Candie reached into her purse and pulled out her phone. Her fingers floated over the phone's screen until she found the object of her search. "Take a look." She pointed a manicured finger at the phone.

My mouth fell open. "How did you find it?"

"I guess since she lives alone, she never thought anyone would snoop through her file cabinet."

CHAPTER THIRTEEN

———

Since I'd left all of my fifty pairs of Dollar Store readers at home, I had to squint at the phone's small screen. I didn't consider the need for glasses a perk of getting older.

I tapped the phone's screen with a fingernail. "This shows proof Calvin blackmailed her. He knew how much Patsy loved Hana as her own child and would do anything to keep him. Would it include murder? This copy of a note from Calvin demanded one hundred dollars, payable before closing time of the shelter every Saturday. I'd say that might give Patsy a reason to kill him."

Candie stared from me to the photo on her cell phone. Lines furrowed her forehead. "But murder? Do you honestly think sweet, quiet Patsy could bludgeon Calvin to death?"

"Listen, she never had children, and she loves Hana like her own flesh and blood. If Calvin threatened to expose Patsy to the authorities for illegally importing Hana, maybe she would hit him over the head if she got scared and mad enough." If faced with someone taking away my Porkchop, who knew what I would do.

Candie's puzzled frown deepened. "But she could have bought a Japanese Spitz from a breeder in this country. Why go to all the trouble to sneak one into the States?"

I hated to admit what I was about to tell Candie. To me, my dog was one of a kind. "Even though Porkchop is a purebred dachshund, it doesn't make him the most desirable of his breed."

"Huh?" Candie asked. Confusion shrouded her face. If the furrows in her brow got any deeper, she'd be able to store her favorite tube of lipstick there.

"The other day while I waited to meet with Doc for my interview, I flipped through a doggie magazine. You know, a vet's office reading material is no different than your regular doctor. The magazines all date from at least a year ago."

Candie waved her fingers at me, impatient for me to continue. "Fine, but what does it have to do with Hana?"

"Certain breeders have a reputation for producing better quality dogs than others."

Candie rolled her eyes. "You mean like a designer dog? You can get a better dog from one breeder as opposed to another? What will they think of next? Make it so you can pick your dog's eye color or the color of his coat? It's plain creepy. Why back in the Holler, we were happy if Rufus could fetch a stick, and we left it at that."

"I agree, but what if Patsy wanted a special breeder in Japan for her choice of dog? It would explain why she might have smuggled Hana into this country and not used a breeder here in the States. Or maybe she had Calvin arrange the smuggling for her?"

Candie's curls bobbled as she nodded in agreement. "So, you're saying if in some way Calvin found out Patsy smuggled Hana into this country or he did the smuggling, he blackmailed her with the information. He could have had some shady connection to the importing for him. Maybe he gave her a phone number to call to get Hana. If the police found out he could deny any knowledge of who or how Hana was brought into this country. It would be her word against his."

"Exactly, and it explains why she didn't have two kind words for Calvin when she found out about his murder. She must have breathed a sigh of relief when she became aware of his death. Her secret remains safe, or so she thinks."

Candie tapped a fingernail on the screen of her phone. "But it also proves that Frank Gilbert isn't the only one with a reason to murder Calvin. What do you plan to do with our newfound info?"

"You're right. Our snooping could get Pookie Bear off the hook and back to warming Gladys's tootsies."

Candie rubbed her hand across her forehead. "Y'all, that's plain nasty. Now I've got to scrub thoughts of Gladys and Frank dancing in the sheets right out of my brain."

"I'm only quoting Gladys. But since someone else had a grudge against Calvin, I'd say it gives Frank, as a suspect, reasonable doubt? I guess I'd better let Detective Johnson know about our latest discovery. It might be important in solving Calvin's murder. What do you think I should tell him?"

"The truth of course. Well, maybe you might want to sugarcoat it a bit. It is his investigation, after all. We don't want to step on his shiny shoes. You're right, though, this could put Frank lower down on the suspect list or at least spread the suspicion around some more. I will send this to your phone, so you will have it when you contact Hunky Hank about this latest development." And ease some of Joe's suspicions about me, too. Candie pressed what I presumed were the appropriate buttons to send the photo to my Easyfone.

"Sugarcoat our find? Candie, this is Pookie Bear's, I mean Frank's life we're talking about. Hank Johnson should appreciate any information I give him to help his investigation. I'm only doing my civic duty." I bit my lip and hoped I'd figure out how to retrieve the photo from my phone to show the detective.

Candie rolled her eyes. "Honey, you are such a babe where men are concerned."

So, I hadn't been engaged eleven times like my cousin, but I felt I could handle Wings Falls' newest detective.

I restarted the Bug and pulled back onto the road. We headed towards Candie's house to drop her off. My day would be busy. I had to go by the vet's and check out why Jeanine and Jacob had shared a late lunch together. Then I needed to stop at the police station and tell Detective Johnson about the new information Candie and I uncovered at Patsy's house. This detecting business was kind of fun. My brain cells jumped. It excited me more than writing about the migrating habits of a Northern Black Bat or some such creature. But most important, I needed to return Bob Spellman's, the editor at Rolling Brook Press, phone call. The possibility of him publishing my book, *Porkchop, The Wonder Dog,* excited me right down to my toes. I just hoped I wouldn't be having my book signings from Wings Falls' jailhouse.

* * *

I dropped Candie off so she could resume the beauty sleep she'd said I so rudely interrupted to go sleuthing with me this morning. More likely she wanted to go back to her fantasy dreams about Mark. Then I swung by the police station on the off chance that I'd find Detective Johnson. The information we uncovered burned a hole in my cell phone.

"Can I help you?" PCO Wanda Thurston, headset clamped around her head, sat behind the bulletproof glass. A smile curved her generous red lipstick-covered lips.

"Ummm…" Why couldn't I find my tongue when I needed it? My fingers could type out an article in record time, but the thought of meeting with Detective Johnson struck me dumb.

"Yes?" Wanda cocked a well-shaped eyebrow at me.

My hands held a death grip on the shoulder straps of my purse. "May I see Detective Johnson? I have some information I thought he might find useful."

"I will check to see if he is free. I remember your face, but I am afraid I have forgotten your name."

"Sam. Samantha Davies."

Wanda flipped a switch on the console in front of her and spoke into her headphone. "Ms. Samantha Davies would like to speak to you. She says she has some information you might want." She looked at me and nodded. "Okay, I will tell her."

"Detective Johnson said he will come right out. Please have a seat while you wait." She pointed to the same uncomfortable, metal chairs I had occupied the last time I'd come here. I will have to talk to Mayor Hogan, or better yet, have Candie, when they are in a romantic mood, put a bug in his ear to seriously look into an increase in the police department's budget so they could buy something more comfortable for visitors to sit on. After all, the general public didn't come here to be grilled for committing a crime. I'm not talking La-Z-Boy recliners, but maybe something with a little more padding to the seat.

The door separating the waiting room from the official part of the police station buzzed open, and my thoughts snapped back to the present. There they were again, the butterflies flip-flopping around in my stomach while Detective Hank Johnson walked toward me. His plaid shirt hugged his toned abs. *Stop it!* I mentally chided myself.

I stood and shook his hand. "To what do I owe this pleasure?" he asked.

"Ahhhhh." Oh, brilliant. How informative on my part. I shook my head to clear my brain and loosen my tongue. "I have some information about Calvin's murder I thought you could use."

He cocked an eyebrow. "Did you remember something from Saturday?"

"No, I spoke to someone who I think had a reason to want Calvin dead." I pulled my hand from his before he noticed the sweat gathering on my palm.

His eyes narrowed. "And how did you come by this information?"

I scanned the busy reception area. People came and went as we stood and talked. "I'd prefer to not say in public."

"Let's go to my office," he said.

Detective Johnson turned to Wanda. "Please." He pointed to the metal door he'd come through a few moments before.

Wanda pushed a button to unlock the door. The detective motioned for me to proceed ahead of him. I assumed we were headed for his office.

"To what do we owe the honor of your visit? Want to check out your new digs when I prove you killed Calvin Perkins?" I rolled my eyes. Sergeant Joe Peters, ugh. He leaned against an officer's desk with his arms folded across his broad chest. The buttons strained on his uniform shirt.

"Doing my civic duty, Sandy, I mean Joe." I couldn't resist. His jaw tightened and red flushed his face. His unibrow furrowed as he frowned. He harumphed then turned back to the officer and resumed their conversation as I walked through the patrol room.

Detective Johnson opened the door to his office and nodded towards a chair in front of his desk. "Have a seat."

I smiled. The same uncomfortable chair, from my last visit to his office, sat across from his desk.

"Something funny?" he asked.

Geez, how observant, but I guess it makes for a good cop. "I was thinking about how uncomfortable the chairs are in this place. Maybe my cousin could convince the mayor to ask

City Council to spring for some chairs to cushion the buns better."

Perfect white teeth showed as he chuckled. "Yeah, I guess you're right. After the town hired me, I brought my own desk chair."

"I don't blame you, Detective. You'd need a good massage after sitting in the city-issued ones after a long day's work." What did I say? I mentally slapped myself upside my head.

A smile tugged at the corners of his mouth. "Volunteering? And please, call me Hank."

Heat crawled up my neck. "No! No way, Hank," I said.

Hank steepled his fingers under his chin. "So, what brings you here today?"

"I interviewed Patsy Ikeda for an article and discovered Calvin Perkins blackmailed her."

Hank's hands dropped to the desk. "And she blurted this out to you? And who is Patsy Ikeda?"

"She's a member of my rug hooking group, Loopy Ladies. We get together on Monday mornings." The heat crawling up my neck now changed to anger and not embarrassment. "No, she didn't blurt anything out, but I have the proof right here." I grabbed my purse off the floor where I had placed it next to my chair. "Love Me Tender" echoed from its depths. I saw it was a telemarketer and pushed disconnect to end my ring tone.

"Love Me Tender?" Hank asked.

My temper settled down. Why was I so touchy around this man? "What can I say? I love Elvis. But right here, let me see, Candie showed me how to bring up the photo she sent me." I studied the buttons on my phone and hoped I'd push the right one.

"Candie?"

I glared at my phone and willed the right buttons to jump out at me. "Uhh, yes. Guess I forgot to tell you she came with me. Drat, now what button did she tell me to push?"

"Yes, you did and why do I get the idea this didn't amount to a normal interview? Here let me try to find what you're looking for." Hank held his hand out for my phone, and I passed it over.

He looked up from my phone. He had retrieved the photo Candie snapped of Calvin's blackmail demand. "Tell me again how you came by this piece of information."

By the tone of his voice, I knew he wasn't overly pleased with the explanation I gave him about my mission to clear Frank Gilbert. "As I said, Gladys O'Malley asked me to help her prove her Pookie Bear, I mean Frank's innocence."

"Pookie Bear?"

"Yeah, I know. Kind of cute, though, don't you think?"

Hank frowned. "Getting involved in a murder investigation is anything but cute. Don't meddle in serious business. Leave it to the professionals. And since you obtained this information without the owner's knowledge it is not admissible in a court of law. You put yourself and your cousin in a potentially dangerous situation for nothing."

I gritted my teeth and stood. I didn't even hold out my hand to say goodbye. "Yes, Detective Johnson, I know murder is serious business. And Sandy Peters wants to pin this one on me." So much for sugarcoating my information. I turned and marched out of his office. I might have let the door shut a little too loudly as I walked straight out of his office and the police station. See if I'd ever share any information with Detective "Perfect Abs" Johnson again.

CHAPTER FOURTEEN

―――

"Porkchop, I don't care how great Detective Johnson's buns might look in a pair of jeans or if he does have a fantastic bod. That man is insufferable."

Porkchop cocked his head. He'd listened to my rant since I'd arrived home ten minutes earlier.

"Can you believe he had the nerve, the colossal nerve, to insinuate I don't know murder is a serious business. I mean it's deadly, after all. Geez, I'm the one who found Calvin with his head bashed in. And Joe Peters would love to pin his murder on me." The more I paced my living room the more agitated I became as I thought about my meeting with the maddening detective. I don't know if I was angrier about him insinuating that I didn't know investigating a murder was dangerous, or if the information Candie and I uncovered couldn't be used against Patsy. At least I was able to point out Frank shouldn't be the only one on the detective's suspect list. Or me if I was on his list, too.

Porkchop yelped and thumped his tail on the hardwood floor.

"All right, true. Technically, you found him. Come on, it's time for your lunch." I patted my leg for my pup to follow me into the kitchen.

Kibble plinked into Porkchop's bowl. I started to straighten my neglected kitchen counter and noticed the pad of paper where I'd written the editor Bob Spellman's name and phone number the day before. I glanced at the digital clock on my microwave—2:05.

"Porkchop, it's now or never. With this phone call, we could be on our way to fame and fortune." I picked up my phone and drew in a deep breath. With shaking fingers, I punched in the number Mr. Spellman had left on my answering machine.

A perky young voice greeted me on the third ring. "Rolling Brook Press. How may I direct your call?"

I told Miss Perky that Bob Spellman—heck he had left his first name so why shouldn't I use it—told me to return his call.

"One minute please. I will check to see if he is available to take your call."

I stood in the middle of the kitchen, listening to dentist office music waiting for Bob—in my mind we were now on a first-name basis—to pick up.

I paced from one side of my small kitchen to the other. "Porkchop, what if he has forgotten about us?"

Before Porkchop could respond, a human voice came on the line. "Ms. Davies, or may I call you Samantha?"

Bob Spellman, the editor from Rolling Brook Press, had picked up and was speaking to me, Samantha Davies. I pinched myself to make sure this wasn't a dream.

"Umm..." Brilliant, my first coherent word. "Sam will be fine, Mr. Spellman." I couldn't bring myself to call him Bob. It might jinx the whole deal. I mean I'm not a famous author, yet. Positive thoughts, right?

"Okay, Sam it is. And please call me Bob."

Bob, Mr. Spellman, *really* wants me to call him *Bob*. He wasn't just saying it yesterday. I had to sit on a kitchen chair before I fell.

"Thank you, Mr. Spellman, I mean Bob. I'm sorry I missed your call yesterday. You said you're interested in my manuscript, *Porkchop, The Wonder Dog*."

"Yes, I did. I found it delightful and refreshing in today's market. Did you model the main character, Porkchop, after any dog in particular? I love the dog's name by the way." Bob chuckled.

I smiled down at my beloved pet who sat on the floor next to my chair. "Well yes, I do have a dachshund named Porkchop. He's been my hero in more ways than one over the years."

"Even better. A real dog behind the series."

"Series?" I leapt out of my chair, hurried over to the sink, and splashed cold water on my wrists, afraid that I might faint. This had been a dream of mine for years, but to hear it from an editor was unreal.

"Why, of course. You proposed it in your cover letter, didn't you?"

"Yes, yes." He had caught me off guard for a moment. "So, what do I do now?"

Bob and I spoke for a few more minutes. He said the company would draw up a contract and email it to me before the end of the week. When it arrived, I should have my lawyer review it. Then if we both agreed, *Porkchop, The Wonder Dog* would hit the bookshelves sometime the following year.

After I hung up from Bob, I scooped Porkchop up from the kitchen floor and hugged his sausage-shaped body close to me. "Porkchop, we'll be famous, maybe even J.K. Rowling famous."

Porkchop's chocolate eyes stared back at me.

"It could happen—you never know." I snuggled my face into his warm neck.

The phone rang. The sound jarred Porkchop and me back to reality.

"What if it is Mr. Spellman? Maybe he has called back to say he's changed his mind?" I placed my little buddy back on terra firma and glimpsed at my caller ID. It read Candie. I hadn't called her since my disastrous meeting with Detective Johnson.

"Hi, Candie. What's up?" Dumb question. I knew what she wanted.

"Don't play coy with me. How did things go with you and Hunky Hank?"

I was still sitting on cloud nine from my phone call with Bob Spellman. "Please don't spoil my good mood," I said.

"Okay, tell me first why you are acting so happy, then we'll get to the fine detective," Candie said.

I rolled my eyes. It was a conversation that could wait for a year as far as I was concerned. "Bob Spellman, the editor from Rolling Brook Press, called and wants to publish my Porkchop book."

She squealed. The sound of her clapping hands floated through my phone. "How wonderful. You deserve to be happy. You've worked on your book for at least forever. Memaw would be so proud of you. Even as a kid you were always making up fabulous stories."

The pride in Candie's voice warmed my heart. She was genuinely happy for me. Tears gathered on the tips of my lashes as I thought of our grandmother. The first week I'd arrive in Hainted Holler for the summer Memaw would pack Candie and me in her Ford station wagon and take us to the nearest Walmart. She'd give us five dollars each from the money she saved selling eggs. We could buy anything we wanted, but it had to be something to keep us busy for the whole summer. From a young age, my cousin would head to the toy section and buy a new outfit for her Barbie. When she got older it was off to the cosmetic aisle for a new shade of nail polish or a teen romance novel. Me, I bee-lined it to the stationery department for a new journal to write my stories in. When we got back to Memaw's farm I'd crawl up into the hayloft of Grandpa Parker's barn and spend hours filling the pages of my new journal.

"I'm happy for you, Sam. But I need to know how your meeting went with the Hunkster."

My happy mood deflated like a week-old birthday balloon. "You can rename him, Horrible Hank, for all I care."

"What happened?" Candie's cat Dixie meowed in the background. Her feline demanded as much attention as my Porkchop.

I related every detail of my unfortunate encounter with the detective to Candie. I knew better than to leave anything out. She could make a monk, sworn to silence, spill the beans.

"So, what's your next step? You're not going to let a little bitty thing like this stop you?"

Since I had returned to a calmer state of mind after my phone call with Bob Spellman, I thought, no, positively, no. I wouldn't let a mule-headed detective stop me from helping Gladys and proving Pookie Bear Frank's innocence. After Candie and I said our goodbyes, I sat at the kitchen table and mulled over my next move.

Even if Patsy did have Calvin help her illegally import Hana from Japan, would it push her to murder him? I mean, how much could the penalty amount to? A small fine? Was it worth letting Calvin dig his slimy hooks into her?

"Let me check what I can find on the internet," I said to the empty kitchen. Porkchop had deserted me. He had trotted off with his favorite squeaky toy, a fuzzy warthog, and settled onto the living room sofa. By the sounds of the squeaks, he had zenned out with his toy. I grabbed my laptop from the kitchen counter where I had left it the night before while I did a late-night eBay web search. I had hoped to score another designer handbag but had no such luck.

I fired up my computer and plugged in a few search words for dog smuggling. I found an article about a famous couple who tried to smuggle their dogs into Australia and a number of articles pertaining to smuggling exotic animals into the country. A guy even stuffed miniature turtles down his pant legs to hide them. That made me squirm in my chair, but info on Japanese Spitz was practically zilch. "Wait. Porkchop, look at this." He dutifully trotted in from the living room with Mr. Warthog clenched in his mouth and looked up at me. "In China, you get the death penalty if they find you guilty of animal smuggling. Do you think Calvin had Patsy so scared she thought our government would do something dire to her, too? Well, maybe not the death penalty, but what about a hefty fine? It could wipe out her pension."

"When I go to the vet's to check on why Jeanine and Jacob were having lunch together, maybe I can ask if she knows anything about Hana and how Patsy managed to adopt him. Do you think I can ask one more time about info for an article I'm writing about Japanese Spitz? I hope that excuse isn't wearing too thin." I picked Porkchop off the floor. He dropped his toy at my feet. I held him so he looked me square in the eyes.

"Porkchop, how would you like a nice bubble bath and a mani-pedi?"

I swear he understood every word I said. He jumped off my lap and raced into the living room as fast as his stumpy legs could carry him. He skidded to a halt and slid his long body under my chintz sofa.

I followed his little rotund body into the living room. I bent down next to the sofa and pleaded with him. "I know you hate to have your nails trimmed and a bath isn't high on your fave list, but please Porkchop. It's for a good cause."

* * *

I finally wooed Porkchop out from his hiding place with a hand full of kibbles. Within ten minutes, after packing my reluctant Porkchop in the Bug, we had arrived at the vet's. We entered the building and approached Jeanine's desk.

"Hi, Jeanine."

She stood with her back to me and tucked patient files on shelves behind the reception desk. She spun around to greet me.

"Oh, hi yourself. What can I do for you? I assume this has to do with Porkchop since he's with you." She nodded towards Porkchop who I cradled in my arms.

"I know your groomer has hours today, and wondered if she could squeeze him in for a bath and nail trimming?" I shifted Porkchop in my arms. He had added on a few pounds. I'd have to cut back on his kibbles. Was it time for the dreaded "D" word, diet?

"Let me check." She thumbed through an appointment book sitting on her desk.

Her pencil tapped the open book page. "You're in luck. If you can wait fifteen minutes, she has a cancellation."

I pointed to the park benches lining the reception area's wall. Light posts and wrought iron benches decorated the room, giving it an outdoor atmosphere. "We'll wait over here."

The entrance door swung open. I turned, and expected to find another customer entering the vet's, but was surprised when Jacob Sorenson swaggered inside.

"Well, what do we have here? Two beautiful ladies?" He flashed his gleaming white teeth at Jeanine and me. "Have I got the deal of a lifetime for the two of you."

Jeanine didn't bother to look up from filing papers into patient folders. She rolled her eyes and under her breath said, "Oh, please."

Jacob sat next to me on the bench. The scent of the cologne he promoted wafted up my nose. I had to stifle a sneeze. I guess he believed in self-advertising. The diamond stud in his ear sparkled. He pulled a lotto ticket fill-in sheet out of his jacket pocket.

"The Powerball is up to forty-five million dollars. Can you believe it? If we all put in fifty dollars each it's a sure win. Want to join in with me?" He leaned in closer. I had to hold my breath before his cologne knocked me over.

I pulled back and tried to escape the full force of the cologne. "Oh, my, a little steep for me, Jacob. I usually do the one-dollar scratch-offs and only occasionally."

He squeezed my leg. "Sam, you need to live a little. What's life, but a big gamble, anyway?"

I removed his hand from my leg. Now, why did I object to his bold move? Only yesterday I acted ga-ga over him. "Sorry Jacob—I'm really not into gambling."

Jacob rose and walked past Jeanine's desk towards the back of the clinic. "Ladies, are you sure you don't want to go in with me on some lottery tickets? Last chance. Don't come crying when I strike it big."

"Fat chance it will ever happen," Jeanine said to his retreating back.

I stared after him. "Does he gamble often?" I asked.

Jeanine nodded but didn't look up from the chart she held in her hands. "From what I understand."

My brain began to spin. *Lotto tickets!*

CHAPTER FIFTEEN

———

"Do you want to drop Porkchop off and come back for him later or wait until he's done with his grooming?"

"Huh?" I'd been so distracted by lotto thoughts it took me a second for her voice to register.

"You must be a million miles away." Jeanine leaned her elbows on the counter, a pen stuck behind her ear. The waiting room stood empty except for Porkchop and me.

"I guess you could say so." *More like a couple of million dollars. So how successful was Jacob in Las Vegas? Did he gamble big time?* I thought. "I think I will wait if it is okay?"

"You said Jacob gambled. Do you mean he's not the big success he makes himself out to be?"

Jeanine slapped the folder she held in her hands onto the counter. "Behind his handsome face he hides a hollow person who thinks only of himself. Don't think for one minute he wants to do you a favor by including you in on the lotto tickets. He is out for himself and no one else."

Phew. If her tongue dripped acid there'd be giant holes etched in the countertop. It was an understatement to say no love flowed between them.

"I saw you and Jacob eating lunch together at Momma Mia's the other day. It didn't look like you enjoyed yourself. In fact, I gathered you and he were arguing."

Jeanine's face scrunched up into a sneer. "I don't consider it any of your business, but I was enjoying a relaxing late lunch by myself when that idiot plopped himself down at my table. You must have seen me when I'd had enough of his arrogance and got up to leave." Boy, did she dislike Jacob.

Porkchop squirmed at my feet. He was not one to wait patiently in the vet's office. I thought now was a good time to change the subject and get to my main reason for coming here:

Patsy Ikeda and Hana.

I put on my most innocent voice. "So, I thought I might write a magazine article about Japanese Spitz. You know, like Patsy Ikeda's Hana. Would Doc Sorenson have any info on them that I could borrow?"

A smile spread across Jeanine's face. "Hana sure is a beauty. He's the only one of his breed that I know of that's been a client of Doc. Patsy loves him like her own child. I'd hate to think what would become of Patsy if anything happened to her dog. It would break her heart or worse."

Now to go in for some dirt. "I read they are considered a national treasure in Japan and only a few leave the country."

Jeanine looked down at a file folder. If she'd stared at it any harder, I swear it would have burst into flames. "Hmmm, really? If I remember, Patsy got Hana as a rescue dog."

"A rescue dog? Sounds strange a breed as rare and valuable as Hana would become a rescue." My brain itched with this information. "The only rescue shelter in the area is, or should I say was, Calvin Perkins'. Do you think Patsy rescued Hana from him?"

Jeanine lifted her head and her gray eyes bored into mine. "I don't know. It's possible, but if I were you, I'd research another breed of dog."

The heat from her eyes practically seared my skin, but I needed some answers. "Do you think Calvin blackmailed Patsy over Hana?" I asked.

Jeanine jerked in her chair. I had hit a nerve. "I don't know. Like I said, if I were you, I'd mind my own business. Now if you'll excuse me, I'm busy." She pushed back her chair and walked over to the standing file cabinet and pulled out more folders.

An older woman pushed open the door to the vet's with her hip and walked up to the counter. She struggled to hold on to the leash of a playful and strong Saint Bernard. I was afraid her dog would knock her over or at least dislocate her shoulder.

Porkchop's ears perked up, and his tail wagged. He thought this new guy was a playmate. "Sorry Porkchop, but I think you're a little too small for that big guy. One swipe of his paw and you'd skid right across the room," I said.

The woman glanced down at Porkchop. "Bruno here

can be a handful, but he is gentle as a lamb. He wouldn't hurt a flea."

I nodded and petted her Bruno. My fingers sank into his thick fur. But my thoughts returned to my conversation with Jeanine. What were the chances someone would give an expensive dog like Hana to a shelter? Slim to none, I'd say. Wouldn't they at least try to sell it first? Could Calvin have illegally imported Hana for Patsy and then blackmailed her? I can imagine him clever enough not to squeeze any money out of her right away. He'd wait until she fell in love with the dog and then pounce. Like most seniors, Patsy probably lived on a pension and her Social Security checks. What if she couldn't afford his payments anymore? True, he's the one who would have initially illegally obtained Hana or at least provided her with the info on how to obtain a Japanese Spitz, but he could have threatened Patsy with anything, and she probably would have believed him. She'd be desperate not to lose Hana. Patsy has a good pitching arm, and *if* the bone Porkchop had chewed on at For Pet's Sake was the murder weapon, she might have swung it with enough force to smash in his skull.

"What do you say? Want to go in on a Powerball ticket? This is your last chance to strike it rich with me."

Jacob's voice yanked me out of my thoughts of sweet, petite Patsy being a murderer. He stood next to me and waved the lotto fill-in sheet. Porkchop growled. I bent and smoothed down the hair on his neck that stood on end. "Shh, Porkchop, it's okay."

Porkchop snapped when Jacob reached out to pet him. "Some fierce dog you have there."

My eyes widened in shock. "I'm sorry. He's never acted in such a way before. If anything, he usually rolls over and lets you pet his stomach."

Jacob flashed his toothy grin at us. "Your dog needs some manners. Ever think of taking him to an obedience class?"

Now the hair on the back of my neck stood on end. He'd insulted my dog. Porkchop usually acted as timid as a mouse. He'd never snapped at anyone before. Maybe Jeanine spoke the truth when she referred to Jacob as a jerk. What if he made up all the stuff about his mega real estate deals and the fortune he'd made as a macho wheeler-dealer from Las Vegas? Calvin blackmailed someone who liked lotto tickets. Could it be Jacob?

Well, I knew of only one way to find out.

I ignored the insult he'd flung at Porkchop. It was time to use what Candie always said the good Lord gave me—my green eyes and big smile. I raised my head and flashed my eyes at him along with a megawatt smile.

"I've changed my mind. I'd love to join you in the Powerball ticket. Who knows, with all of your financial good luck maybe some of it will rub off on me and we'll win?" I even batted my eyelashes at him. Candie would be so proud of me.

I opened my purse and took out my black flowered Vera Bradley wallet. I unzipped the bill section, prepared to dodge the moths about to fly out. Thank heavens for Ms. Visa and Ms. Mastercard. An advance on my book contract couldn't come soon enough. A career as a freelance writer was fine, but the pay didn't amount to much. My income from the funeral home covered monthly bills and a few extras, like my yen for designer handbags. I hid some cash in my sock drawer at home for emergencies. I figured my attempt to prove Frank and myself innocent fell into that category.

I zipped my wallet and tucked it back into my purse. "I must have left my extra money at home."

"No biggie. Why don't we meet at Sweetie Pie's?" Jacob peered at the large gold watch encircling his wrist. "At say six thirty, and we can settle up the fifty dollars then?"

"Fine with me. Porkchop should be finished with his grooming, and I will have time to go home and get the money for our winning lotto ticket."

He let out a loud laugh. I must amuse Jacob. I squirmed in my seat. He sounded like a donkey braying. Why had I, and half of Wings Falls High, ever thought him handsome? His laugh alone turned me off. Youth overlooked so many things. I guess his laugh would have been small potatoes when you considered most of us had had zits populating our faces.

Porkchop growled when Jacob turned and left. "Yeah, I know, not the Mr. All American we—or should I say 'I'—thought."

"Porkchop? Porkchop Davies?" A cinnamon-colored woman in her twenties stood at the door to the interior of the building. She propped it open with a sneaker-clad foot. Dogs and cats romped across her scrubs.

Porkchop's ears twitched forward at the sound of his name. "This is Porkchop," I said and walked towards her.

She held out a slim hand to take Porkchop's leash. "Hi, I'm Kim, the groomer."

"Sam, Porkchop's owner," I said. "I thought about waiting, but I think I will pick him up later." I turned to the desk to mention this to Jeanine but found it empty. "Could you tell Jeanine to give me a call when he's finished?"

Kim scooped Porkchop into her arms. "Sure, he'll be the most handsome dog in Wings Falls when I'm finished." By the way his tail started to wag at warp speed, he liked what Kim had said. Exactly what I needed—my dog with more attitude than he already had.

I stepped out of the vet's. The day had turned warm. I might have to put the top down on the Bug. I opened the car door, and my nose began to twitch. A foul smell smacked me in the face. Had I forgotten to take something into the house the last time I'd gone grocery shopping? Maybe it had turned rancid in the warm car. I'd have to do a thorough search when I got home. I sat in my seat and powered down the windows. My foot pushed down on the gas pedal only to feel it squish into something soft. I scanned the floor and found the source of the pungent odor—dog poop. How did it get there? But more importantly, why? I rolled my eyes upward and spied the answer to my question.

A note taped to the visor read: *Mind your own business or next time you'll be up to your neck in this stuff.*

CHAPTER SIXTEEN

———

"Ugh, if I hadn't bought these shoes only last week, my feelings would be more scared than mad." My fingers poked under the passenger seat for the pack of Wet Ones kept there for sticky-hand emergencies. I flung open the driver's side door, twisted in my seat, and flicked off the offending shoe. "Geez, this dog doo sure smells ripe." I sucked in my breath, held the shoe at arm's length, and swiped at it the best I could. I shook my head at the results. My newly purchased shoes were history, stained beyond repair. Right now, if it was revealed to me who had planted the dog poop, it would do my heart good to add them to the morgue's body count. Then I'd turn myself in for murder to Detective Johnson. My reason for committing murder—I'd claim temporary insanity. Not a jury in the country would convict me once they saw the damage done to these beautiful leather shoes.

I groaned. "Now for the car floor. I'll do my best to wipe it up. On the way home I can stop by the car wash and give it a good scrub." I peered up at the note still taped to my visor. "I will deal with the note once I get home and call Candie." Crime doesn't run rampant in the North Country, so people felt safe to leave their car doors unlocked or at least it hadn't until recently. Maybe I had better start locking my car when I leave it unattended.

With my rear end hanging out the car door, I scrubbed at the gas pedal and surrounding area. When finished, I stuffed the soiled Wet Ones into an empty plastic grocery bag, scrounged from the floor of my back seat and tossed it in the metal trash can sitting outside the vet's office building.

The sound of "Love Me Tender" jolted me out of my thoughts of murdering whoever did this. My caller ID indicated the number belonged to the vet's. Wiping up the car's mess took longer than I had thought. I hadn't even made it out of the parking lot. I flipped open my phone and answered. Jeanine informed me Kim, the groomer, had finished Porkchop's mani-pedi.

Jeanine looked surprised to see me as I pushed open the vet's heavy glass door. "Wow, you got here quick."

"Umm, I got sidetracked in the parking lot." I lifted my stained shoe and waggled my foot back and forth.

Jeanine's eyes rounded and her nose wrinkled. An obvious dog doo odor still clung to my shoe. "You didn't step in something did you?"

I nodded, but gave no details. I wanted to keep what had happened in my car to myself for the moment. "That bad, huh?"

Jeanine huffed out a big breath. Her bangs flew off her forehead. "I don't know what's wrong with people. We have a roll of doggie doo bags hanging by the trash can in the parking lot so people can clean up after their dogs, but they still let their dogs litter the sidewalk. People."

"I hear ya." I shook my head and sighed. "These shoes were bought only last week. I scored them at a sale The Clothes Horse was having. The bottoms aren't even scuffed." That store was a favorite of mine, especially when they had their designer handbags on sale. Oh, who was I kidding? I loved any bargain I could get there.

"Well at least you hadn't left the parking lot, yet," Jeanine said. It didn't look like she'd made a dent in filing the pile of patient charts on her desk from when Porkchop was dropped off.

"No, trying to clean up the mess took a while." My mad still clung to me, or as Memaw Parker used to say, "I was madder than a hen in a sack."

Jeanine picked up the phone that sat on the counter. "Right," she said. "I will let Kim know you are here."

After collecting Porkchop, I sat in the Bug in the vet's parking lot and dialed Candie's number. She didn't pick up, but I left her a message on her voice mail about the present left in my car and the accompanying note. Next, it was a drive to the Wash and Wax to scrub the Bug's floor mat the best I could, but my efforts didn't meet Porkchop's standards. He jumped into the back seat and hung his head out the open window all the way home. Not normal behavior for him, as he usually curled up in the passenger side and fell asleep as soon as his long torso hit the seat. I attempted to do the same, hang my head out the window as I drove, but after two near collisions, I sucked in my breath and braved the car's parfum d' dog poo. This reminded me of the doggie/owner perfume Jacob had displayed at the vet's. If he was such a successful real estate magnate in Las Vegas, why did he need to make a few bucks selling perfume? Hmmm, maybe it'd be one of my questions to ask him at Sweetie Pie's.

I turned into my driveway and saw Candie sitting on my front porch. She leapt off the porch swing and ran towards me as soon as I pulled the Bug to a stop.

My dear cousin whipped open my door and folded me into a bear hug. "Are you okay?"

Porkchop jumped and yelped from the back seat.

Tears welled in my eyes at the concern she showered on me. Her body trembled about as much as mine. The seriousness of the threatening note started to sink in.

Candie tugged me towards my front porch. Porkchop trotted along behind us. "Let me see it." Once we were settled on the white wooden swing, with Porkchop curled at my feet, she waggled her fingers at me. "Come on, come on."

"Okay, okay, give me a chance to dig it out of my purse." I zipped open my brown C-patterned Coach bag and fished into the side pocket where I had tucked the warning note.

When it hit the light of day, Candie grabbed it out of my fingers. Her brow furrowed and her hands began to shake as she read it. Lips set in a grim line, she said, "When I find out who this egg-sucking dawg is, their butt is grass and I'm the lawnmower."

Oh geez, Candie had her Southern up—she was madder than Memaw Parker's wet hen. A cardinal Parker family rule, you didn't mess with kin.

"Now Candie, maybe it's not as bad as we think. We could be reading more into this note than is there." Family loyalty became a blind spot with her. I didn't want her doing anything foolish for my sake.

"Not as bad as we think." The rhinestones on her blouse bounced with her rising temper. I swear steam came out of my cousin's ears.

My finger touched my lips. "Shhhh." I peeked at Gladys's house to make sure Candie's outburst hadn't attracted my neighbor's attention. All I needed was Gladys catching wind of me receiving a threatening note and all of Wings Falls would know.

Candie shook the note at me. "You have to let Detective Johnson know about this right away."

"Do I have to?" I sounded like a whining toddler, but the last thing I wanted to do was tell him about the note. He'd give me another lecture about the dangers of a murder investigation and tell me to butt out. But this was my life, and I didn't need Joe Peters clamping a pair of silver bracelets on my wrists.

"Yes, and right now." Candie pulled out her phone and punched in some numbers. She held the phone to her ear then spoke to the person who answered. "Yes, Samantha Davies here, could you please put me through to Detective Johnson. It's important."

She thanked whoever answered on the other end and handed her phone to me.

While I waited to be connected, I asked, "How did you know the police station's number?"

She gave me an "You cannot be so dumb" look and said, "I work at the mayor's office, remember. I have to know those kinds of things."

Duh, of course, she did. The mayor's office and the police department worked hand-in-hand.

"Detective Johnson here. How can I help you?" His voice jerked me back to the present and the reason for the phone call. I related to him my dog doo incident and the note left in my car visor at the vet's.

"I need to talk to you about this note ASAP." His clipped voice told me my dodging a lecture wasn't an option. I informed him that Candie and I had an appointment shortly. I would call the station when I was finished to make sure he was still available.

My hand shook as I handed Candie back her phone. Not from fear this time, but anger. "How dare he use such a tone of voice with me," I said between gritted teeth.

"Sam, he's only doing his job. He's a good detective. It's the reason why Wings Falls lured him away from Albany PD. Now, what's this appointment we have?"

I told her of my suspicions about Jacob, and that I'd arranged to meet him at Sweetie Pie's for dinner.

"Can you come along with me? I don't want to eat with a possible murderer by myself. We will tell him you wanted in on the lotto action, too, and wanted to rub the lotto ticket with your hand for good luck.

Candie nodded in agreement. "Smart thinking. Until the police solve this murder, you shouldn't meet with any suspect alone. Especially, since you received a threat. You've hit someone's raw nerve."

Porkchop jumped onto my lap, and I stroked his head. "Jeanine mentioned Jacob might not be the big Las Vegas wheeler-dealer he makes himself out to be. What if she's right? I mean why would he push the perfume? And what is with wanting to get people to go in with him on a lotto ticket? On Calvin's list he did blackmail someone with a lotto connection. Could it have been Jacob?"

"I will text Billy Bob to find out what he can dig up on Jacob." Candie's fingers flew across her phone's small screen. How could people send messages so fast? Punching the tiny phone numbers on my flip phone challenged me more than I wanted to admit.

My forehead wrinkled in confusion. "Billy Bob?"

"You know, my ex-fiancé. He is a PI in Vegas, and he'd do anything for me."

I laughed. "Which one was he?" My cousin may have gotten engaged—and unengaged—eleven times, but she remained friends with all her exes.

Candie smiled. "Number five. We had a lot of fun. When do we meet with murder suspect number two?"

I glanced at my watch. "In about fifteen minutes. Let me get Porkchop settled, change my shoes, and grab some money."

"By the way, how much will this lotto ticket cost me?" Candie called after me.

"Fifty dollars," I shouted from inside my house.

"Fifty dollars! This murder has become expensive," she said from the porch.

Yeah, I thought, *I hope the price doesn't include my life.*

CHAPTER SEVENTEEN

———

"Take a table wherever you like, or should I say wherever you can find an empty chair," Franny Goodway said over her shoulder. With a row of plates balanced up her arm, Franny navigated her way through packed tables and booths.

Candie and I had entered Sweetie Pie's, and the place hopped with the dinner crowd. The evening had remained warm, and the blast of air conditioning flowing through the café was delicious against our hot skin. The sweet scent of baked goodies mixed with barbecue and sweet potato fries tickled my nose.

"Sam, over here."

My eyes sought out the voice, and I found Jacob ensconced in a booth at the rear of the diner. He waved his arm to attract my attention. He wore a pale green Ralph Lauren polo shirt with the collar turned up. Is the flipped-up collar still in style? I remembered it as a fad in high school. Maybe it was a Las Vegas thing, and the retro fashion statement hadn't reached Wings Falls, yet.

We tried not to knock into any of the wait staff serving hungry customers as we wove our way through the tables to Jacob's.

"I got here early and was starving so I thought I'd go ahead and order a bite to eat." A plate with a half-eaten pulled pork sandwich, complete with a side order of fries, sat on the red Formica table in front of him. Sweetie Pie's served up pulled pork many declared better than sex. At least it's how people have described it to me, though I wouldn't know, since I'd climbed on the abstinence wagon five years ago.

He swiped a barbecue-stained paper napkin across his mouth and pointed to the booth bench across from him. With grease-covered fingers, he motioned for us to sit.

"Heathen," Candie said out of the side of her mouth as we slid into the booth. Jacob broke one of Memaw Parker's cardinal rules of etiquette: a gentleman stood when a woman approached a table. If nothing else, Memaw drilled manners into her grandchildren. A good way to get her dander up, act disrespectfully. She said the world might be changing, but manners would always remain important. They showed what kind of upbringing your folks gave you.

"Good evening, Jacob. I don't know if you've met my cousin, Candie." My jaw clenched as Jacob's eyes traveled over my shapely cousin and settled on her well-endowed bosom. *Scum,* I thought.

"Ladies, how you doing today?" Franny stood next to our table holding two glasses of ice water. Beads of water dripped down the sides. "You plan on ordering some dinner? Your partner here has a head start on you." She nodded towards Jacob. I got the impression Franny and Memaw came from the same mold. For Jacob to eat before we arrived was a definite no-no in their Southern book of manners.

I wanted to concentrate first on questioning Jacob before we ordered our dinners. "Let me think for a few minutes about what my stomach hankers after, okay?"

"Sure, take your time." Franny's eyes circled the busy café. "Not like I have nothing to do." She placed the water glasses on the table. She turned and left when another diner called her name.

I focused my attention on Jacob. "I told my cousin about the lotto ticket you want me to go in on, and she said she'd like to join us, too. Right, Candie?"

By the way her foot tapped the linoleum floor underneath the table, she still was not a happy camper with Jacob's lack of manners. I poked her in the ribs to bring her back into the conversation.

Candie blinked. "Um, what?"

I glared at Candie. "The lotto ticket. Remember, the one Jacob said if we each pooled fifty dollars we'd have a great chance of winning big money." Would Candie mess up my opportunity to question Jacob about Calvin's murder? How else could I prove Frank Gilbert's and my innocence if I couldn't pin down the possible murder suspects who Calvin blackmailed?

"Oh, yeah," Candie said in her best Southern drawl. She leaned towards Jacob and cocked her head. "So, sweetie, little ol' you want to make us all millionaires?"

I coughed and gagged on a sip of water. Candie would win an Academy Award with this performance.

"You all right?" Candie pounded me on the back.

I grabbed a paper napkin out of the metal container sitting on the end of the table and sputtered into it. "Fine, fine," I said.

"So, tell me, Jacob, honey, how many millions do you think we'll win?"

I couldn't believe it. Candie batted her eyelashes at Jacob. He ate it up. He sat with his mouth open, and a half-eaten sandwich poised midway to his mouth. Any minute now I thought he'd slobber into his pulled pork.

Jacob shook his head to break the spell Candie had woven around him. "Yeah, yeah we'll stand knee-deep in the big bucks when we win."

Candie reached across the table and squeezed his arm. "Oh, I do like how you talk. So positive and everything."

I sat there, my eyeballs rolled towards the ceiling. I might as well have been invisible. Candie held Jacob mesmerized.

It was time to pull the conversation back to our original purpose, Calvin's murder, and possible suspects of that terrible deed. "Jacob, I understand you're promoting a new doggie/owner fragrance. Did you concoct it in Las Vegas? You still live there, don't you?"

Jacob's eyes snapped towards me. "Um, yes, I live there. But I'm in town paying my brother a long-overdue visit. You know how it is, one gets caught up in life and time slips away from you." Jacob puffed up his chest. "I've been so busy building my real estate empire in Vegas that visits to my big brother have been very few over the recent years. I told my secretary to clear my calendar then hopped on a jet and headed home for a much-needed visit. I brought some of my doggie perfume with me in order to judge how it would do back East. It's a hit in Vegas."

Candie stared wide-eyed at Jacob. "How marvelous. I mean, you've become so successful. Imagine coming from a small town like Wings Falls. I guess one could say you struck it rich. It makes you sort of a local celebrity. Oh, oh, speaking of celebrities, do you meet many celebrities in Las Vegas?" she said. She bounced in her seat and fluttered her eyelashes at him again.

I had to give it to my cousin. She sure knew how to stroke a man's ego. I imagine, with all those exes, she had lots of practice.

Jacob leaned across the table. In a voice barely above a whisper he said, "I don't like to brag, but I had dinner with Adele right before I flew East. And Wayne—it's Wayne Newton I'm talking about—well, I've sold him a house or two."

"You have?" Candie asked, wide-eyed. Her mouth hung open in amazement. "Wayne Newton and Adele? I love them." She added a wiggle of excitement on the bench seat for effect. "Could you ask her for her autograph for me? I'd treasure it forever if you could get it for little ol' me." My cousin reached across the table and squeezed Jacob's hand. He tugged at his collar. I swear sweat beaded on his forehead as he gazed down at her hand.

A pinging bounced around the inside of Candie's purse. "Excuse me, honey, I'm expecting an important text, and this might be it." Candie zipped open her purse and pulled out her rhinestone-studded cell phone. As I've said before, not too much escapes Candie's love of bling. I swear when she does make it to the Pearly Gates, she won't put one step through them unless Saint Peter hands her a set of wings decked out in rhinestones.

Candie peeked at her phone then at me. Her eyes sent me a secret message. "Samantha, dear, I'm having a little case of the vapors. Do you mind escorting me to the ladies' room?"

Jacob's brow furrowed. "Can I be of any help?"

"No, darlin', I only need to splash a little water on my wrists, and I will be fine. When we get back, we'll finish our conversation about how you're going to make us all gazillionaires." Candie gave his hand another squeeze.

"What happened out there? Are you all right?" I said as soon as the ladies' room door swished shut behind us. The bathroom, meant to hold only one person, became a little cramped with two of us huddled inside. Not to mention how two persons in a one-man/woman john might raise a few eyebrows.

Candie shoved her phone at me. "Hush and read this."

"What?" I squinted at the phone. I had left my Dollar Store glasses in my purse, back at the table.

"It's from Billy Bob. He found some things about Mr. Big Shot Las Vegas out there." My cousin cocked her head towards the door.

I looked at the phone and scrolled through the text. The more I read, the tighter my hand clenched her phone and the more the rhinestones dug into my palm.

"Arrested for assault? Up to his ears in debt? Being investigated for land deal scams? Possible ties to a Vegas mafia? Is there anything criminal he's not involved with?" My head spun from reading Billy Bob's text. "If he's done all this in Las Vegas, would bumping off a small-time blackmailer be beyond him?"

CHAPTER EIGHTEEN

———

I handed Candie her phone. "We'd better return to the table before Jacob wonders what's keeping us. I've got some serious questions to ask him."

Candie tucked the phone into her purse. "Any suggestions on how we go about grilling him, so he won't get suspicious?"

"I'm not entirely sure but follow my lead in whatever I say." I pushed open the bathroom door and reentered the restaurant. The sound of clanking dishes and diners' voices bombarded my ears after the relative quiet of the bathroom.

I slid back into the booth and smiled at Jacob. I hoped to lighten our upcoming conversation so he wouldn't become suspicious.

He looked up from his plate. A piece of pulled pork clung to his pinkie finger. "Everything okay, Candie?"

Candie waved her hand to dismiss that anything was wrong with her. "How sweet of you to ask. I'm fine. A momentary case of light-headedness came over me."

"Glad everything is all right. I never could figure out why women can't go to the john by themselves." Jacob laughed then coughed. Shredded pork flew across the table and landed next to my water glass. "Oops, guess some pulled pork slid down the wrong pipe."

Any remaining teenage image I had held of him looking like a football hunk became permanently scrubbed from my mind.

"Jacob, I'm surrounded with that scent of the new perfume you're promoting, everywhere I go. It must be catching on. Of course, I smelled it at your brother's place, but I also got a whiff of it while I waited for you the other night at Momma Mia's."

Jacob's face split into a grin. "Yes, it's taken off and selling like crazy. You know how people love their pets. They'll buy anything to help them identify with the bundle of fur they love. Remember the old saying, people eventually start to look like their pets? Well, I'm hoping they'll want to smell like them, too."

I lifted an eyebrow. I wouldn't say I would want to smell like Porkchop especially when he comes in out of the rain. Nope, smelling like a wet dog didn't appeal to me.

Jacob laughed. "Oh, I mean only in a good way. One spritz of my doggie/owner perfume and dogs and their owners will be in seventh heaven."

I wrinkled up my nose in a sniff. "Do I detect it on you now? That scent smells familiar."

Jacob leaned over the table. "Here, take a whiff." He thrust his neck towards Candie and me.

Candie wasn't the only Academy Award winning actor in the family. Hollywood must have placed an Oscar in the mail for me, too. I held my breath so I wouldn't gag. A peek out of the corner of my eye showed me Candie had the same problem. I knew I would owe her big time for this one.

"Ah, Jacob, how…interesting. Does it have a name? I mean if I want to buy some, I'd like to know what to ask for." I'd become BFFs with my ex's wife before I would splash his perfume on myself. I had too much respect for my body.

Jacob paused in mid-bite of his sandwich. "Yeah, I've named it, Poochie Love. I mean, who doesn't love their dog. I'm working with a fellow to develop one for cats, too. The world is filled with a bunch of crazy cat ladies who would snap it up."

Oh, no. I felt Candie's back become rigid in the seat next to me. Her Southern was flaring up again. Malign her or her cat, Dixie, and you'd better duck. The South was about to rise again. I needed to do something and quick to ward off her first shot.

"Candie, what a delight! You and Dixie can smell like sweet things together." I knew she'd as soon dine with a mean 'ol polecat than splash Jacob's perfume on her porcelain white skin.

"You know Jacob, I also think I caught a hint of it Saturday morning when I dropped some dog food off at Calvin's shelter." I studied him for his reaction. He didn't disappoint me. Jacob dropped his pulled pork sandwich on his plate and started to cough.

He swiped a napkin across his mouth. "Something must have gone down the wrong way again. Umm, yeah, he carried some of my perfume at the shelter. I cut him a deal. Part of the sales' profit would go to benefit the shelter, kind of a donation."

Donation my foot. If he'd donated a penny to anything but himself then Porkchop's winning the next Nobel Peace Prize.

Candie shifted into her Scarlett O'Hara role again. "Honey, how nice of you. I'm sure Calvin appreciated your kind offer."

Prodding Jacob, I asked. "The scent I smelled was pretty strong. What if someone walked down the hallway wearing your perfume right before I got there? What do you think? Geez, maybe the killer left right before me."

The color drained out of his face. He made Candie's case of the vapors look like a minor itch. "Jacob, here, take a sip of my water. You look like you're about to pass out." Jacob's water glass was empty, so I pushed mine across the table towards him.

"Ah, thanks." He clutched the glass and sipped some water. "Calvin's murder must have upset me more than I thought."

I cocked an eyebrow. "I didn't know you two were so close."

"I wouldn't say close, but he was a good man and didn't deserve to die the way he did." Jacob gulped down the rest of the water.

I didn't think Calvin deserved to die either but calling him a "good" man stretched it a little.

"You ladies ready to order?" Franny stood next to our table, a pen poised over her order pad.

"Franny, you do walk on quiet feet. I didn't hear you come up to our table," I said, picking up the menu I already knew by heart.

Franny laughed. "Yeah, I am pretty light on my feet. It's amazing what you can learn when customers don't know I'm standing right next to their table."

Jacob's head jerked toward Sweetie Pie's owner. "Really?" Red flushed up his neck.

Franny tapped her pencil on the order pad. "Yep, but my lips are sealed. Wouldn't be good for business if I spread all the town's gossip, now would it?"

"I imagine your customers have buzzed about Calvin's murder," I said.

Franny nodded her head. "Buzzing like bees around a honeycomb. I understand you discovered his body. What a sight to behold."

"Not one Porkchop or I ever want to repeat." I had to ask, "Any speculation amongst the busy bees as to who did it or why?"

"Now, Sam, I already said I'm not one to spread gossip, but..." Franny looked over her shoulder then back. "You know Calvin wasn't the most loved character in town, some people even say he had some shady dealings on the side."

I ventured a question to observe Jacob's reaction. "Do you think he tried to extort money out of people? I know he always needed money for his shelter. Jacob even said he donated money from the sales of his new perfume."

Franny squinched up her forehead. "Extort? What do you mean?"

I peered at Jacob out of the corner of my eye before I laid the "B" bomb on Franny. "You know—blackmail. Maybe he had some information that a certain person didn't want revealed and he blackmailed them. That person couldn't take it anymore and, they snapped."

Jacob bolted upright in his seat. My hunch paid off. I'd hit a nerve.

"Blackmail? I never would have thought of blackmail, but you could be right. Money is the motive for many murders. At least I see it on my television police investigation shows. Now, enough gossip. I'm breaking my own rule here. What do you ladies want to order?" Franny poised a pen over her pad.

"How about a burger with all the fixin's?" I ordered then turned to Candie.

"I will have the same but hold the onions. Mark said he might stop over later," she said. A smile curved her Passion Pink–covered lips.

Franny called our order to Joe, the diner's assistant cook. While Franny liked to prepare a lot of the orders herself, she also loved to mingle amongst her customers. She had schooled Joe on how to cook as "Southern" as herself.

Time to go in for the kill. Oops, bad choice of words. I leaned over the table and spoke in a hushed tone to Jacob, "Do you think Calvin blackmailed people? That could have turned dangerous, deadly even."

"Umm, couldn't say." He took a glimpse at his gold watch. "Geez, look at the time. I forgot I have a phone conference with my investor in half an hour." He slid out of the booth and pulled his wallet out of his jeans back pocket, then flipped open the worn leather wallet and peered inside. "Would you mind picking up the tab? The smallest I have is a hundred-dollar bill. I will pay you back the next time I bump into you." Jacob stuffed his wallet back into his jeans pocket and hurried from the diner. He barreled into a waitress on the way to the exit causing her to spill a tray full of drinks. He didn't even send an "I'm sorry" her way.

I frowned at his retreating back. "Well, what do you make of his hasty exit?" I asked.

"You mean how he stiffed us for his lunch? Smallest he had was a hundred-dollar bill, yeah right." Candie glared as Sweetie Pie's door shut behind him.

"No, ninny, how he acted like I had poked him with a red-hot stick. He couldn't get out of here fast enough when I mentioned the word blackmail."

"You know, you are right. It is like you set his britches on fire. And he did not even help the poor waitress he plowed into. Such a clod. Did you notice, he completely forgot about the Powerball ticket?" Candie clapped her hands in excitement.

"I guess we did get off cheap enough if we only have to pay for his dinner and not fork over fifty dollars each for a ticket," I said and grinned. I patted my purse knowing I would go home a little richer.

"Hi, Candie. Hello, Sam."

I looked up. Jeanine stood beside our booth

"Hi, yourself, want to join us? We've ordered our dinners, but only a few minutes ago." I figured this might present another opportunity to find out more about Jacob.

"Afraid I can't. I am on my way to Fair Oaks to spend some time with Momma. She loves Franny's pecan pie. I wanted to surprise her with a piece." It was hard to compare Jeanine, the perky teenage cheerleader from high school, with the woman who stood next to my booth, her mousy brown hair pulled back in a braid dangling down her back. Gone were the miniskirts and close-fitting T-shirts from our teenage years. Baggy slacks and a rumpled blouse hung on her rail-thin body now. Where was that bubbly girl? What had happened to her to cause such a dramatic change?

"Have a seat while they box up your pie." I pointed to the bench vacated by Jacob. "How is your mom nowadays? I know she used to be such an active member of her church. Always leading Bible study groups."

Jeanine slid into the bench. "She does miss being as active as when she attended her church. But her Bible gives her great comfort. She believes it word for word. I think I disappointed her when I didn't take to it as she did." She stared down at her hands and picked at a hangnail.

I nodded my head in agreement. "I know what you mean. I'm sure at times when growing up I had let my parents down, too."

Jeanine looked up and stared off into space. "Not like I did. At least my seven siblings made her proud."

I reached across the table and placed my hand on her arm. "Oh, I'm sure you did, too," I said.

"The Bible says 'go forth and multiply.' Well, not me, and Mom never lets me forget it." Jeanine snapped back into focus. "Her pie is probably ready. I've got to go." She jumped up and scurried over to the cash register.

CHAPTER NINETEEN

———

I stared at Jeanine's back as she hurried out of Sweetie Pie's. "Did I say something wrong?"

Franny had delivered our orders, and my stomach delighted in the juicy burger I sent its way.

Candie shook her head. "Darned if I know. She and Jacob both suffer from burning britches."

"Maybe she wanted to get the pecan pie to her mom as soon as possible. I do remember from high school, her mom acted demanding. When Jeanine was cheerleading at a game you could hear her mom in the bleachers shouting at her to cheer louder or perform a better cartwheel. I didn't think much of it at the time, other than the fact that I was thankful my parents didn't embarrass me that way. Maybe I was lucky being a nerd after all. I didn't have to perform before most of the school like Jeanine. It doesn't sound like her mom has changed much since our school days." I thought back on memories of my parents. They may live a distance from me now, in their condo in sunny Florida, but a girl couldn't have two more loving and caring parents than I.

I swirled a french fry into a glob of ketchup. "Speaking of Jacob's burning britches, what do you make of his quick exit after I mentioned Calvin possibly blackmailing people?"

Candie lifted her burger with pinkies up. You'd think she was drinking tea out of a fine china cup. "He ran out of here faster than a hot knife cuts through butter."

"He sure did. And he paled whiter than Memaw's sheets when I mentioned smelling his perfume at the shelter the morning of Calvin's murder. I'd say it positively puts him on the suspect list for Calvin's murder." And me further down that list. I bit into my burger. Drat, a blob of ketchup landed on my white T-shirt. Back in the day, when I cared, George always complained about how I constantly spilled food down the front of me. He threatened to buy me bibs to wear when we dined out. Maybe since I didn't live up to his preppy standards, he used it as an excuse to do the mattress dance with his dear Anna. I dipped a paper napkin into my water glass and scrubbed at the spot. It didn't do much good, other than smear the stain more. I would have to make a quick change before I stopped to meet with Detective Johnson and talk about the doggie poop and show him the note left in my car.

"So, let's see. We have Patsy Ikeda, afraid of losing her dog, Hana. There's Jacob Sorenson up to his ears in deep doo in Las Vegas if Billy Bob's info turns out to be correct. And unfortunately, we can't eliminate Frank Gilbert." I swirled another fry into the ketchup and popped it into my mouth. "I want to believe he's innocent—I mean he's Gladys's Pookie Bear, after all. But even the most innocent person could kill someone if pushed hard enough."

"Pookie Bear?" Candie asked, dabbing a napkin to the corners of her mouth. As I said she's a real Southern lady, unlike her Northern cousin. It's not as if Memaw didn't drill manners into me when I visited Hainted Holler, but you'd never find Candie in a T-shirt and yoga pants let alone jeans. But she might sport a pair of cowboy boots under her frilly dresses and skirts. She does have sort of a wild side. For sure, rhinestones would stud her boots.

"Didn't you ever have pet names for any of your eleven exes?" I remembered calling George "Sweets," back in the day. Now I can't repeat what I call him. In my youth, I'd have gotten a good soap scrubbing of my mouth for even thinking such language.

Candie grinned. I could tell she was taking a trip down memory lane. "Well, I do remember calling one of my ex-fiancés Cuddles, and there was Honey Bunch. A wide smile spread across her freckled face. "How could I forget Lovie Toes?"

"Lovie Toes?" I laughed. Soda snorted out of my nose.

"He had the most gorgeous toes and when we, you know, snuggled, he would entwine them with mine and oh my! Well, enough of my reminiscing." Candie blushed and snapped back to earth. Her trip down exes lane was over.

I held a hand over my mouth. My cousin had always parted on friendly terms with her exes and my finding humor in their nicknames wouldn't settle well with her. "Do you call Mark anything special?"

"At the office, when we're around others, he's Mr. Mayor. Otherwise, it's Mark."

"What about when you are alone, no Honey Pie, Lovey Kins, or Poopsie?" Now I laughed out loud.

Candie glared at me. She didn't recognize the same humor in the situation that I did. "No, Mark, or Mayor Hogan," she said. "Enough about my personal life. Let's try to solve this murder so we can prove Frank, Pookie Bear, or whatever you want to call him, innocent."

"And stop Joe Peters from harassing me about Calvin's murder," I added.

"Love Me Tender" jangled in my Coach purse. I dug my phone out and checked the caller ID. George, my ex. I should block him, but we're still partners in The Do Drop Inn Funeral Parlor. He only called when he needed something done, and it was usually not anything I wanted to do. His phone call surely would not benefit me.

Candie noticed my frown. "Who is it?"

I sank in my seat. She wouldn't like my answer. "George," I said, in a hushed voice.

Candie sat up straighter in the booth and tried to snatch the phone from my hand. "Don't answer the dog."

I pulled the phone out of her reach. "I have to. It might have to do with the business."

"He can leave a message," she said, gritting her teeth.

I shook my head no and flipped open the phone. "What do you want, George? I'm busy right now." I may have to answer my phone, but it doesn't mean I have to be polite.

I listened to what he had to say then groaned. "I'm sorry, George. It completely slipped my mind about babysitting Harry and Larry this weekend so you and Anna can go on your mini-honeymoon." I silently gagged. Visions of him and his sweet-tart dippity-do-dahing all weekend invaded my mind.

Candie sat close enough to me to eavesdrop on his end of the conversation, too. She poked me in the ribs and mouthed *No*. Unfortunately, in a weak moment, when I had called the funeral parlor to ask why my monthly partner's check was late, I had agreed to care for his twin boys while he and Anna spent a weekend romping in the Adirondack Mountains. The children were the reason he so proudly left me for Anna after he got her pregnant. I didn't blame the little guys. They didn't pick their parents, and they are sweet boys. They even call me "Aunt Sam." They weren't responsible for their idiot father.

My back stiffened. Resolve flooded my spine. He wasn't going to use me as a doormat anymore. "Sorry George, but I'm tied up right now and can't take care of the boys this weekend. Can you ask if Anna's mom will babysit them? Or better yet take them with you. They'd love a weekend in the mountains."

"What?" Could the whole diner hear him shouting? "Take kids on a honeymoon? Are you nuts?"

Now the gloves came off. "Excuse me, if my memory serves me right, you put that baby cart before the old horse five years ago." I flipped my phone shut before he could reply.

"You go, girl!" Candie held her hand up for a high five.

I grinned and slapped it good, but then my grin wavered. "It's not the boys' fault their father acts like a toad. They are great kids. Porkchop and I even enjoy their company."

"Sam, don't you even go there. Finally, you are standing up to El Jerko. Plus, we have a murder to solve."

I nodded. Candie was right. "I need to get over to the Wings Falls Police Station and show Detective Johnson the note someone left in my car. Do you think I should give him the Black Book we found in Calvin's office, too?"

"Yes, I do. This is getting more serious by the moment. Someone knows you are digging into Calvin's murder. The killer threatened your life. They have killed once. You may be the next victim." Candie motioned for Franny to come over to our table.

I shuddered. "Aren't you being a little melodramatic? Who'd want to kill me?"

Candie drummed the table with her manicured fingernails, impatient with my naïve attitude. "The same person who killed Calvin and does not want to be caught."

Burger and fries churned in my stomach. I had never thought of it that way. I only wanted to help a little old lady prove her Pookie Bear innocent. And clear my name with Joe.

"Ladies, you ready for your bill?" Franny pulled the tattered receipt book out of her lace-trimmed apron pocket. "I notice your dinner guest left and stiffed me."

"Don't worry we will take his slip, too." I pulled my wallet out of my purse.

The smooth brown skin of Franny's forehead wrinkled. "Hmm, some gentleman." She sniffed the air like she smelt something rotten.

Candie nodded. "I agree."

"You know you asked me what folks said about Calvin's murder? Well, I will break my rule to tell you this. The morning of his murder Jacob came rushing in here. In a real state, too. He plopped onto a stool by the counter and demanded a mug of coffee. 'On the double' he said to me. I don't know who he thought he was talking to. So, I poured him a mug of coffee, but his hands shook so bad he could hardly even hold it. He kept looking at the door as if he was expecting someone."

"My, that sure is strange. What had he seen to make him so riled up?" Candie asked, searching her purse for her wallet.

"Only one thing I know happened Saturday morning that could upset someone so much, Calvin's murder," I said, digging through my wallet for my share of the bill. And oh, yeah, half of Jacob's bill.

When Franny left our table, I turned to Candie. "Do you think he could have murdered Calvin? I mean, what else would have him so upset?"

"When you were at the vet's, could he have overheard you asking Jeanine questions about him? He's always hanging around there. Maybe he heard you and put the dog doo in your car?" Candie fished in her wallet for what she owed of our bill.

"Hi gals. Thanks so much for the help at the shelter the other day. I don't know what I would have done without you."

I glanced up from my wallet. Shirley Carrigan stood next to our table. "It was nothing. Glad we could help. You know small towns—people are always willing to pitch in when you are in need."

Shirley grunted. "We're talking about Calvin. He didn't endear himself to people, small town or no."

I waved my hand. "No big deal." I eyed her outfit. She wore a spandex top and pants, workout clothes. "Coming from the gym?"

A fine sheen of perspiration dotted her forehead. "Yeah, it helps me keep my mind off what's been happening at the shelter. I stopped in for a bite to eat before I head back to For Pet's Sake to tend to the animals."

I pointed to Candie's and my clean plates. Only a few crumbs remained of our burgers. "Sorry we can't join you. We've finished. And as usual, it was a great meal."

"No problem. There's a vacant stool at the counter I can grab. I wanted to stop to thank you for your help." Shirley turned and walked towards the empty counter stool.

I grabbed Candie's arm. "Do you see what I see?"

"What, what? Oh, I do now." Candie nodded.

Her eyes widened when she spotted it. A jump rope dangled out of the gym bag slung over Shirley's arm.

My stomach churned. Jump rope—a clue from Calvin's Black Book. Was Calvin such a sleaze he'd blackmail his own girlfriend? He certainly wasn't any prize, but I didn't think even he would sink that low.

CHAPTER TWENTY

———

"I know, I know, Porkchop. Candie will do worse than kill me. She'll have a flying duck fit. I'd say if she were an earthquake, she'd register higher than ten on the Richter scale."

Porkchop sat next to me on the sofa and cocked his head. He stared at me with his liquid chocolate eyes. "I couldn't face a meeting with Detective Johnson, not after our dinner with Jacob Sorensen. Anyway, it was late by the time I dropped Candie off at her place. It was practically six thirty."

Woof, woof!

Was Porkchop channeling Candie and reprimanding me for not stopping by the Wings Falls Police Station after our dinner?

"Okay, so maybe it is a feeble excuse. To be honest, and this is between you and me, Porkchop. I could not stand the thought of another lecture from the good detective. Scoot over. You are lying on my wool strips." Quarter-inch strips of blue wool lay in a pile on the sofa next to me. I had neglected my hooking since my Loopy Ladies' meeting yesterday morning. My seascape rug was stretched across my frame. I wanted to escape to the beach with my hooking. True, this was only Tuesday evening, but I tried to do a little hooking every morning and possibly squeeze some into the evening as well. The mindless pulling of wool loops relaxed me.

Porkchop's ears perked up. He jumped off the sofa and scurried toward the front door. He acted better than any security system. Seconds later my door knocker rapped against the door.

I eyed my Timex and saw it was seven o'clock. "Now who could that be?" I asked myself and placed my rug hooking frame on the floor then pushed off the sofa. I joined Porkchop at the door. Odd, he didn't bark, and his tail wagged. I peered through the door's peephole, then groaned.

"Traitor," I said, glaring down at Porkchop.

I pulled open the door. "What can I do for you, Detective Johnson?"

Detective Johnson stood on my front porch with his thumbs hooked into the front pockets of his jeans. One of his signature ties, this one with an image of George Jetson zooming through space, hung loosely around his neck. And the dratted brown curl my hands itched to smooth back, lay against his forehead. "Since you didn't come by the station today like you said you would, I thought I'd stop by and find out what you wanted to tell me."

Caught. I heaved a large breath and slowly exhaled it. "My day was exhausting. I wanted to come home, relax and hook for a while."

One of his well-shaped eyebrows rose. Stop it, I chided myself. Who cares what his eyebrows look like? "Not what you are thinking. I rug hook for relaxation. I would have come by tomorrow. Anyway, Candie's the one who thinks you should see the note. It's no big deal."

"I was in the neighborhood. Why don't you show me this note and let me be the judge of how serious it is? May I come in?" Detective Johnson pointed towards my entryway.

Short of being rude, I couldn't think of a single reason why he shouldn't come in. Otherwise, he would probably get a search warrant or subpoena me or take a battering ram to my front door. All right, so I was letting my thoughts run towards the dramatic, but I did not want to talk about my close encounter with the possible murderer at the vet's right now. I had successfully pushed it to the back of my brain for the evening and wanted to zone out with my hooking.

I pushed open the screen door separating us. Porkchop did a happy dance at the detective's feet. "Traitor," I mumbled again under my breath.

Detective Johnson bent and scratched Porkchop between the ears. He immediately flopped on his back for a belly rub, Porkchop I mean, not the detective. I smiled, in spite of myself, as I imagined the detective squirming on the floor, anticipating a belly rub.

"Something funny?" he asked. He walked beside me into my living room. Porkchop jumped at his feet.

Geez, he didn't miss a thing. I needed a quick answer. "I like your George Jetson tie."

Detective Johnson fingered his tie. "Yeah, I was in a Jetson kind of mood this morning."

I motioned for him to have a seat on the sofa. "You must have a large collection of cartoon character ties."

"Every Christmas and birthday I get a couple." He sat at one end of the sofa while I cleared my hooking off the other and joined him.

I swear Memaw whispered in my ear to be a polite hostess, because before I knew it my mouth was moving, and I offered him something to drink. "Would you like a drink, Detective? A cold beer, iced tea, or a glass of lemonade?"

"Please, call me Hank. I know we didn't get off on the right foot. I may have acted a little hard on you at the station the other day, but when you are involved with as much crime as I, you know not to deal with murder lightly. Truce?" The detective, or should I say Hank, held out his hand for me to shake.

"Truce." I slipped mine into his large, calloused hand and we shook. "A couple of microbrews from the new brewery in town are chilling in my fridge. How about one?"

"Sounds great. Tonight is a hot one. Doesn't the weather start to cool down in the Adirondacks once the end of August hits?"

"It usually does. The weather has remained unusually hot and dry this summer. It might affect the number of leaf-peepers we get this fall," I called from the kitchen. Porkchop bounced at my feet. He expected a treat to drop his way. I couldn't resist his pleading eyes. I gave in and tossed him a nugget. So much for my resolve to take the waddle out of his walk. Tomorrow was another day.

"Leaf-peepers?" Hank said from the doorway to my kitchen. He leaned against the door frame while I reached into my refrigerator for two beers.

"Oh right, you are not from the area. Leaf-peepers refers to the tourists who travel north in the fall to observe the trees change their colors. With the lack of rain this summer, the leaf colors won't be as vibrant. It's a big deal since this area depends on the tourists. The local businesses rely on tourists' dollars to survive." I popped the top of a beer and handed it to him. Then I pulled a glass out of the cabinet next to my fridge and held it out, but he waved it away.

I didn't want Hank to think I was a wimp, so I flipped the cap off my beer and drank from the bottle, too. Nothing better than the taste of a cold beer sliding down your throat on a hot summer evening.

We wandered back to the living room and reclaimed our seats. Porkchop trotted along with us. He jumped up and scooted next to Hank. The detective scratched my disloyal dog's back with one hand and clutched the beer bottle in the other. The lock of brown hair my fingers itched to push off his forehead, caught my eye again. I squeezed the neck of my beer bottle until my knuckles practically turned white to curb my impulse.

"So, do you want to show me this note?" Hank rested the bottle on his muscled thigh.

"One second, I will get it." I stood and walked into my bedroom to retrieve the note. While my hand dug into my Coach bag and found it, my fingers also brushed against Calvin's Black Book. *Should I, or shouldn't I?* I pondered the wisdom of showing him the book, too. After all, if you want to get technical, I probably was withholding evidence. Was I acting a wee bit picky, maybe? I mean, the police had their chance to find it when they searched Calvin's office. It wasn't my fault I was luckier than them. But my biggest fear? The wrath of Candie. I didn't want to hear from her if I failed to turn it over. Before I could change my mind, I grabbed the book out of my purse, found the note, and headed back to the living room.

I felt a smile spread across my face. Hank sat on the floor tossing Porkchop his favorite ball. Maybe the detective had a few redeeming qualities. My dog certainly took to him.

Hank rose from the floor and sat on the sofa again. I sat too, but folded my legs underneath me. Porkchop jumped onto the sofa and curled up next to Hank. "Here's the note I found taped to my Bug's visor." I leaned towards him and handed it over. "But that wasn't all the culprit left behind." I filled him in on the gift of dog doo left on the floorboard.

Was I mistaken or did the detective's jaw clench as he read the note? His hand stilled from scratching Porkchop. "The murderer, and I'm going to assume it's the person who placed this note in your car, has unquestionably, made a serious threat. He wants you to stop poking your pretty little nose into things."

I blinked. Did he say I had a pretty nose? Oh please, Sam, he only wants you to butt out. Remember, you are at least ten years older than him.

"I know, but I have to help Gladys. I promised her." I did not want to see the disappointment on her face if I told her I couldn't help prove Frank innocent. And I wanted to wipe the smug look off of Peters' face when he finds out I didn't have anything to do with Calvin's murder, either.

"I'm sure she doesn't expect you to put yourself in danger while you try to get Frank off the hook. It's my job." Hank folded the note in half and tucked it into his shirt pocket.

I fidgeted in my seat, and Hank eyed me. "Is there something else?"

"Ummmm, when Candie and I helped Shirley Carrigan at the shelter the other day, you might say we kind of found something." I held the Black Book out to him.

Hank reached for the book. "What's this?"

I twisted my hands in my lap. "We, I mean Candie and I, kind of think Calvin blackmailed people. He wrote in the book in some sort of a code. Maybe one of them murdered him? Blackmail would be a big motive."

Hank opened the book and thumbed through the pages. "Peanuts, lotto tickets, aspirin, binkies, jump ropes?" His brow furrowed into a frown.

"Yeah, my cousin and I have deciphered at least two of the codes, maybe three. We are certain the word *peanuts* refers to Patsy Ikeda, and we attribute *lotto tickets* to Jacob Sorensen. *Jump ropes* could mean Shirley Carrigan. At least three other people could have had a reason to kill Calvin besides Frank Gilbert." Excitement threaded through my voice as I laid out my theory.

He tucked the book into the back pocket of his jeans. "Very interesting, but playing Nancy Drew could get you and your cousin killed. You should have handed this book over as soon as you found it. Withholding evidence can get you arrested."

I'd had it. I rose from my seat and put my hands on my hips. "Are you threatening me, Detective?"

"No, only a warning. You are playing with fire, and you could get burnt."

I walked towards the front door and flung it open. "Thanks for the warning, Detective, but I'm a big girl and can take care of myself."

He sighed and trudged to the door. Porkchop followed along behind him. Hank touched my nose. "Remember someone doesn't want you poking your pretty nose into this murder investigation." He bent down and gave Porkchop a parting scratch between the ears then pushed open the screen door and left.

I slammed the door shut after his retreating back. "I've had it, Porkchop. You can forget about your new BFF. If he thinks I am going to stop now he has got another think coming."

I grabbed my cell phone off an end table and hit the speed dial button for Candie's number. She answered on the second ring. I didn't give her a chance to complain on the off chance I had interrupted a date with Mark. "Candie, come to my place at nine tomorrow morning. We're going to flush out suspect number three."

CHAPTER TWENTY-ONE

———

"If you say one more word about my not going to the police station, I will pull over to the side of the road and you can walk home." I peered over at Candie. My cousin jutted out her bottom lip like a sulking child. She knew I had a head of steam going and didn't want to risk a hike home in her stilettos.

"I'm only saying you could have avoided all this nastiness with the detective if you'd gone to the police station as I suggested."

I blew out a puff of air. "Okay, I will admit I should have gone, but after our dinner with Jacob, I was too worn out."

Candie giggled. "Did Detective Johnson say you had a cute nose?"

My face reddened at the thought. "Yeah, he did."

Candie clapped her hands. "I knew it, I knew it. He's attracted to you."

"Yeah, when Lake George freezes over in June," I said, which usually didn't happen until January. "Anyway, how many times do I have to tell you, I'm too old for him?"

"Too old? Nonsense!" Candie reached in her purse and dug out her cell phone.

"Who are you going to call?" I glimpsed at her out of the corner of my eye.

"Shirley. I think it would be better if we tell her we are coming than show up unannounced." Candie scrolled through her contact list and hit Shirley's number.

I braked for a red light. "How come?" I drummed my fingers on the steering wheel, waiting for the light to change.

Candie pushed back her curls and placed the ringing phone to her ear. "Well, we need to give her an excuse as to why we're there, so we don't make her suspicious of our real objective."

I pursed my lips in thought. "Right. We don't want to put her on the defensive by accusing her of murder. At least, not right away. So why would we go to the shelter? I don't have an extra bag of kibbles to donate. How about we tell her we'd like to help some more with putting Calvin's office in some kind of order? Especially, since we didn't make much of a dent the other day."

"It might work. We're at loose ends today and thought maybe we could help. The office area is a mess and I think beyond her right now." The sun sparkled off the rhinestones on the cell phone Candie held to her ear.

She held up a finger as the call connected.

"Hi, Shirley. This is Candie..." Candie relayed our excuse for a visit then hung up.

"What did she say?" I asked. The light turned green. I pulled into the right-hand lane and headed towards the shelter.

"She's over the moon for our help with Calvin's office. You heard me mention the cleaning company you use at the funeral parlor can't fit her into their schedule any time soon, so we wanted to volunteer our help again. Shirley said she's had her hands full with the animals and hasn't done a thing in the office."

A few minutes later, the three of us stood in the hallway outside Calvin's office. Shirley flung open the door. "Where do you want to start? I haven't set foot in here since you left the other day. I've got enough to do just feeding and caring for the animals." The fast-food wrappers still littering the desk and floor gave credence to her words.

"How are you doing? Have the volunteers been allowed back in?" I walked over to the desk and picked up a crumpled burger wrapper. I shoved it into the trash can next to the desk.

Shirley twirled a strand of hair between her fingers. "Thank heavens, yes. I don't know what I'd do without them. These poor animals don't know what's happening. They still need to exercise, have their cages cleaned, and get their tummies fed."

My hand swept the room. "From what Candie and I saw the other day, I think we can trash most of this stuff. Do you have a large plastic bag?"

Shirley nodded. "I will go fetch one." She turned and left the office.

Candie kicked trash out of the way as we entered the office. "So, what's our plan? How do we get her to open up about her relationship with Calvin?"

"Hmmm, I will think of something—follow my lead." I shuddered and looked around the office. I should have brought rubber gloves. My skin already began to itch as I thought of all the germs running rampant in this room. For sure, I'd have to take a hot shower after we tackled this mess.

Shirley entered the office and held out a black bag. "Will this do?"

I motioned towards the litter-filled room. "That bag is fine. We will make a start on this mess. Can you stay awhile in case we have any questions about what we're tossing out?"

Shirley glanced towards the doorway. The sound of barking dogs drew her attention. "I guess so. A volunteer arrived a couple of minutes ago. He can start feeding the animals."

I smiled in an attempt to put Shirley at ease. "Great. I figure you'd probably know better than Candie and me what's important for the business. Right, Candie?"

"What?" Candie jerked to attention. I think she'd drifted off to a Mark Hogan dream world again. Did my cousin know how bad the love bug had bitten her this time?

"Yeah, for sure, Candie said. You'll know a good deal more about how the shelter is run than us."

Shirley shrugged her shoulders. "Don't know how much help I am able to offer. Like I said the other day, Calvin became secretive about this place, the business end at least."

I peered at Shirley as I shoved the fast-food wrappers into the trash bag. "Why do you think he acted so closemouthed about the shelter? I mean, he did a great service for the animals of Wings Falls. You would think he'd want all the publicity he could get. It would help raise funds for the shelter."

"Didn't Patsy Ikeda get her Hana here?" I picked up a burger box. Mold sprouted fuzz on the bottom. Yuck, I will have to double soak my body after I dive into this filth.

Shirley smiled. "Yes, she did. I remember when she got Hana. What a special day for her."

"She loves the dog like her own child. I guess in a way he is," Candie said, scooping up a pile of papers.

Shirley chewed on a fingernail then walked to the door and shut it. "It took a while for Calvin to get Hana for her. Once when he'd had too much to drink, he told me he had to pull a few strings to get the dog." She stooped to pick up a crumpled piece of paper off the floor.

Time to stop beating around the old bush. "Do you think he blackmailed Patsy?"

The paper Shirley grasped in her hand fluttered to the floor. "He may have. She'd come by every Saturday. I'd thought at the time maybe she had dropped something off. You know, like the dog food Porkchop didn't like?"

"What makes you think differently, now?" I bent, grabbed a hamburger wrapper, and shoved it into the black trash bag.

"Well, for one thing, Frank Gilbert came every Saturday, too. Then one day I opened the mail and a check for one hundred dollars from Jacob Sorensen fluttered out. All the way from Las Vegas. What was even stranger, an envelope with one hundred dollars cash arrived the same day, too. No note indicating the sender, only two fifty-dollar bills," Shirley said.

Candie picked up a folder of papers she had abandoned on the floor the other day. "Did you ask Calvin about the money?"

Shirley shook her head. "I did, and boy did I regret it, too."

"How come?" I followed the hamburger wrapper with a stack of empty takeout coffee cups.

"His face turned beet red, and he started throwing things at me. Shouting at me that I should keep my hands off his mail and never go near it again. Luckily, I have quick reflexes. I ducked fast enough not to get hit. I took off and went to the women's shelter for the rest of the day." She nodded at Candie. "The shelter is a blessing."

Time now to ask the question nagging at my brain. "Did he blackmail you, too?"

Shirley's face paled. I had my answer.

Her bottom lip trembled. "How did you know?"

"It looks like Calvin kept a record of those he blackmailed." I looked around the room. "His office might look a mess, but he kept accurate records of his victims. He used code names, and one of them he called Jump Ropes. We figured it might be you."

Shirley started to sway. Candie and I raced over to grab her before she could collapse on the floor. We led Shirley over to the office chair. I brushed off the papers scattered on it and guided her to sit.

Tears trickled down her face. Her voice trembled. "Yes, Calvin blackmailed me, too. But not in the way you might think. He used, I figure what you'd call, emotional blackmail. You see before I came to Wings Falls, I had a career as a female wrestler." Candie and I both nodded. "Well, fame and money can do some pretty serious damage to your ego if you don't know how to handle the pressure. And I didn't." Shirley's words came out in gasps. Tears appeared to clog her throat. "I ranked at the top of my league, a champion. Some guy from New York City got ahold of my manager and convinced him if I threw a championship fight, he'd set me up for life with money."

"Didn't you have any say in this?" I asked.

"What did I know? A poor kid from the Bronx. I'd never had so much money before in my life. And what was one fight anyway? I could reclaim my title with the next fight." Shirley pulled a crumpled tissue out of her jeans pocket and blew her nose.

I laid a hand on Shirley's shoulder for comfort. "So, what happened next? How could Calvin blackmail you about the fight?"

"I threw the fight, but an investigation followed. They found me guilty and drummed me out of the league along with issuing a hefty fine. I moved here to Wings Falls and tried to put all of those memories behind me. I was so devastated and lonely. One day, I came to Calvin's shelter to look for a pet as a companion, and the rest became history."

Candie knelt next to Shirley and folded her hands in hers. "But how did Calvin find out about your past?"

"I fell in love with him or so I thought. He acted so good and kind to the animals in the shelter that I thought it reflected his personality. One night, after we made love, I poured my heart out to him. I told him everything. Stupid me."

Shirley shook her head. "He used what I told him to keep me tethered to him. He said if I ever tried to leave, he'd find me and spread my story to whomever would listen. It makes sense now, Jacob and the others who sent him money."

"What do you mean?" I asked.

Shirley let out a deep shuddering sigh. "Well, at the end of the month he'd say to me 'You are paid up for this month.' I thought he was referring to my part of our apartment rent he had deducted from my paycheck. Guess, it was his inescapable hold on me about my past he talked about."

Candie squeezed her hand. "You are right. You became a prisoner tied to him by your past."

Shirley stared up at me. "You don't think I killed him, do you?" Panic etched her face. "He may have made my life a living hell, but I couldn't kill anyone. Not even a dirtbag like him."

I pulled Shirley into a hug. Sobs shook her body, and her tears soaked the shoulder of my blouse. Deep down I knew she couldn't have killed Calvin, but if not Shirley, then who did?

CHAPTER TWENTY-TWO

———

"Okay, we've questioned Patsy Ikeda, Jacob Sorenson, and Shirley Carrigan. We've solved the code names: Peanuts, Lotto Tickets and Jump Rope. But we still haven't figured out Aspirin or Binkies."

Candie and I sat in my living room sipping chamomile tea. Porkchop lay dozing beside me on the sofa. My free hand idly stroked his long body. After we had quizzed Shirley about her relationship with Calvin, we stayed to help clean up his trash heap of an office. We were guilted into it after the emotional wreck we'd made of Shirley. We carved a fair size dent into putting things in order. At least McDonald's and Burger King no longer comprised the major decorating elements of the room.

Candie propped her feet up on the battered wooden trunk I used as my coffee table. "Much as you don't want to, we need to question Frank Gilbert."

"But he's such a sweetie. He'd never hurt a flea. Besides, I don't want to face the wrath of Gladys if she doesn't like the questions I ask." With my hands wrapped around a Harry Potter mug, visions of an avenging Gladys defending her Pookie Bear floated around my mind. My hands trembled at the thought.

Candie peered at me over the rim of her mug. "What's the matter? You look scared out of your wits."

"Imagine Gladys if she thought I accused her Pookie Bear of murder." Porkchop stirred but continued his soft snoring. His ears twitched as he slept.

Candie shook her head. "What a scary thought. Do you think you'd come out of it alive?"

"Place my ashes in an urn, and put me on the captain's chair next to Gladys's husband. We can stand guard over the neighborhood. Promise me you'll take care of Porkchop." At the mention of his name, Porkchop opened one eye and stared at me. Since I hadn't mentioned the word *treats*, he closed it and floated back to dreamland.

"Oh stop. You'll do fine. Besides, you know my baby pussy cat, Dixie, and Porkchop don't get along. I can imagine it now, the stare downs and fur flying. It would be World War III at my house if the two of them lived together. So, if for no other reason than for Porkchop's safety, you have to survive that interview." Candie placed her mug on the trunk and started to rise.

"Won't you come with me? There's safety in numbers." I hoped begging would get Candie to relent and come with me.

She smoothed down her skirt. "I pleaded with Mark to have this morning free so we could go to the shelter. I don't dare ask for the afternoon off, too. I may date him, but when we're at the office everything becomes professional. If he knew how involved I am in this investigation, let's say he wouldn't be thrilled." Candie reached for her purse sitting on the floor next to the sofa.

I gave her my best sad eyes. "All right. I don't want you getting in trouble with Mark."

My cousin laughed. "Those eyes may have worked on Memaw, but they don't do a thing to me."

"Brat." I got up from my sofa and reached out and hugged her.

She stood beside me with hands on her hips. "What did Memaw used to say when things got tough?"

Together we repeated our grandmother's favorite chant. "Always remember you are a Parker and can do anything you set your mind to." We dissolved into a fit of giggles.

Porkchop jumped off the sofa and leapt around at our feet, barking. He probably thought his mistress and auntie were acting crazy.

I showed Candie to the door then walked back to my dining room. Porkchop trailed behind me.

I slapped my forehead. "Darn, how forgetful of me." The contract for *Porkchop, The Wonder Dog* sat on the table. What was with me? Bob Spellman from Rolling Brook Press calling was the most exciting thing to happen to me. Well, maybe the second most exciting. Finding a dead body kind of topped the list. I needed to find a contract attorney ASAP. Surely attorneys had a network and the funeral parlor's attorney, Stanley Silverman, could recommend someone. This would go on my to-do list right after I talked to Frank. On second thought, maybe a call to Stanley should top the list. Was I procrastinating? Yep, big time. Even more important, I didn't want to face Frank to ask him if he murdered Calvin—and most of all the possible wrath of Gladys.

I peered down at Porkchop who sat at my feet. "What do you think, Porkchop?" I picked up my cell phone and held it in front of me. "Frank or Stanley?" Porkchop barked twice. "Okay, Stanley it is." I scrolled through my contact list and punched in his number. After two rings his secretary answered. I relayed to her my dilemma of needing a contract attorney. She said Stanley was in court, but she'd be sure to pass my message along to him.

"Double drat. No putting it off any longer. Time to talk to Frank." Porkchop stared at me with his warm brown eyes and cocked his head. I peeked out my side window. Frank and Gladys sat on her front porch. An idea struck me.

"Porkchop, want to go for a walk?" He bounced up and down on his four stubby legs then darted to the front door. "Who can get mad with a cute little doggie like you at my side?" Boy, using my dog as a shield. Did this hit a new low or what?

Frank waved. "Beautiful day, isn't it? How's my buddy Porkchop doing?" Porkchop's tail wagged at the mention of his name.

"Will you join us for a spell?" Gladys asked.

"Yes, thank you. It is a beautiful afternoon." I climbed the wooden porch steps and sat on the top one. Porkchop sniffed at the bushes edging the porch. He went into his chipmunk scouting mode. Paint peeled off the house's clapboard siding and a shutter hung drunkenly from a downstairs window. The house showed its age like the owner and her Pookie Bear.

"Would you like a glass of lemonade?" Gladys asked, rocking back and forth on a wicker rocker.

"I would love one, thanks. It is extremely hot for this late in August." I had hoped to get some questions in to Frank while Gladys went in the house to fetch my glass of lemonade. Talk about being chicken. I checked to see if my arms had sprouted feathers.

"Be back in a minute." Gladys pushed off her rocker and retreated into the house. The wooden screen door slammed shut behind her. A smile spread across my face.

"What fine memory are you lost in?"

Frank's words brought me back to earth. I chuckled. "You could say I am. The sound of a wooden screen door shutting always reminds me of summers at my Memaw Parker's in Tennessee. My cousin, Candie, and I ran barefoot and free all summer down there, dashing in and out of our Memaw's house."

Frank nodded. "The past sure can hold some mighty fine memories. 'Fraid the present not so much."

This was my opening. I sucked in a big breath and went for it. "Frank, did Calvin blackmail you? Is that the reason you drove to the shelter on Saturday morning?"

The screen door flew open and slammed against the porch wall. Frank's avenging angel stood framed in the doorway. Her hand shook so hard the lemonade sloshed over the rim of the glass. "Samantha Davies, what do you think you are doing asking my Frank such awful questions? He has nothing to be ashamed of. He's a fine upstanding man."

Porkchop, startled by Gladys's forceful entrance onto the porch, leapt up the steps and huddled on my lap. I pulled him close to me to calm his trembling body.

Frank stared up at Gladys with weary eyes. "It's all right, Sweets. You asked Sam to help clear my name, so she has a right to ask questions." He leaned forward in his wicker chair. His gnarled hands hung between his legs. He stared at the worn porch floor as if trying to gain strength from its old oak boards. After a few seconds, he heaved a deep sigh and sat back in his chair.

"I've tried to be the upstanding man you think I am, Gladys, but the truth is I wouldn't say my past has always shown brightly." Frank ran a hand through his thinning white hair then turned and looked at me. "To answer your question, Sam, yes, Calvin blackmailed me."

A loud gasp escaped Gladys's lips. "I don't understand. You said you went to the shelter on Saturdays to make a donation."

Frank let out a bitter laugh. "Donation? Yeah, I guess

you could call it a donation. A donation to the Calvin Perkins Fund of Greed."

Porkchop had settled down. He snored softly on the step beside me. "Why did he blackmail you?"

A spasm of pain passed across Frank's face. "It's not something I'm proud of. Back when I attended veterinary school, my mom got sick. My folks needed money real bad to help with her medical bills. I had access to the meds we gave the animals. The school was lax about securing them or so I thought. So, I figured, why not take a few to sell? A druggie could get as good a high off them as any meds prescribed to humans. I thought I'd only take a few. Just enough to help my folks with their bills. Well, dumb me, I didn't know the school had hidden security cameras in the room. The first time I tried to swipe the pills, I got caught. Since it was my first offense, and with extenuating circumstances, I didn't get jail time, but probation. Oh yeah, and kicked out of school."

Gladys reached over and caressed Frank's hand. "It's okay, Pooks. Desperation will make us do strange things. We all do foolish things when we're young."

Frank gazed at Gladys with such tenderness that I became uneasy for intruding on such a personal moment.

"How did Calvin find out?" I asked.

"About five years ago, I began volunteering at his shelter. From the little I knew of him, I thought he was an okay guy, what with all the animals he cared for. Guess he figured I knew a little too much about cats and dogs to be only a veterinary tech. He phoned a friend who worked at Cornell. The guy did some snooping around for him and dug up my past."

I shook my head. "Some way to repay you for helping him out at the shelter."

A lone tear trickled down Frank's face. "Calvin demanded a hundred dollars a week. Due on Saturday." He turned red-rimmed eyes up to Gladys. "It's why I went there last Saturday morning. But I swear I didn't kill him. I might have hated his guts, but I couldn't kill anyone. Not even a low-life like Calvin."

"I know you couldn't, Pookie Bear." Gladys leaned over and hugged Frank.

"It must have been your car I heard squeal out of the parking lot."

Frank looked up in confusion. "Huh, what? No, it couldn't have been me. I stopped by the shelter early on Saturday, about six o'clock. I worked an early shift at the animal hospital. Calvin was alive and well when I left." Frank pulled out of Gladys's arms. "I can prove it by my punched timecard at the vet's."

"And you didn't leave at any time?" I asked, pushing him a little harder.

"No, not until my shift ended at four." His eyes pleaded with Gladys to believe him.

How could I not believe Frank? He said Calvin was alive when he left the shelter. But I also found it hard to think of Patsy and Shirley as murderers, too. Jacob, well maybe, though behaving like a jerk didn't necessarily make you a murderer. Heck, if acting like a jerk was the criteria then they would have locked up my ex years ago. And thrown away the key.

Since *aspirin* was a name of a drug, I bet Calvin used that term when he referred to Frank. I was left with only one more suspect, Binkies. Who belonged to this code name? Was this the person who murdered Calvin?

CHAPTER TWENTY-THREE

———

I chugged an iced tea. The ice cubes looked so inviting I wanted to pour them over my head. Summer was hanging on for all its worth. Candie and I sat in a booth, eating lunch at Sweetie Pie's. I filled her in on my meeting yesterday with Frank.

Candie took a sip of her lemonade. "Frank has an alibi as to his whereabouts for Saturday morning?"

My cousin was so unaffected by our late August heatwave, I wanted to kick her under the table. Not a curl on her head frizzed from the humidity. Me? Even with the restaurant's air conditioning humming full blast, sweat, or as Memaw Parker would have said, dew, plastered my tank top to my body.

"Yeah, at least three other people working at the animal hospital can confirm he was there. Gladys, though, sure wasn't happy with me. Her claws came out when she overheard me questioning Frank. And to make me feel even more like a heel, he hadn't told her the reason for Calvin's blackmail. In fact, she didn't even know that Calvin was blackmailing him. She thought Frank made his Saturday morning trips to For Pet's Sake to make a money donation to help Calvin out."

Candie rolled her eyes. "Yeah, Frank was helping Calvin out all right, but not because he wanted to."

Elvis Presley's "Hound Dog" played over the sound system. Waitresses scurried about delivering lunch orders. Hot air drifted into Sweetie Pie's every time the front door opened announcing another customer's arrival or exit.

Candie swirled the ice cubes in her lemonade with a straw. "So, you believe Frank is innocent?"

I nodded. Hair had escaped from my ponytail and hung limply around my face. "I do. If you saw the sorrow and regret etched on his face as he explained why Calvin blackmailed him, you would, too. My heart ached for him. He was a desperate young man trying to help his family."

Candie frowned. "Has your fondness for him influenced this decision?"

Shaking my head, I said, "No, my gut instinct tells me he didn't murder Calvin."

Candie picked at the BLT our waitress had set in front of her moments before. "Where does that leave us? Back to square one as to who whacked Calvin. Maybe a stranger killed him. You know a random killing."

"What do you mean random killing?" Trying to be a little more conscientious about my food choices, I poked at a Caesar salad. The shorts I'd tugged on this morning were definitely tighter than the last time I had worn them. Although, thinking about it, they may have shrunk in the wash. Yes, it had to be the answer. I smiled to myself and doused my salad with dressing.

Candie stabbed the air with her sandwich. "What if someone driving by the shelter could have killed Calvin? You know, maybe a druggie thought the shelter had cash lying around."

I frowned. I had never thought of a druggie angle to Calvin's murder. "Do you think it could have happened that way? We've followed all the clues in Calvin's Black Book. All of them except Binkies. I can't imagine what the name refers to. You might be right. Calvin's murder could be a robbery gone bad. Maybe Calvin surprised someone trying to steal money from his desk. The burglar grabbed the first thing he could get his hands on, the dog bone, and hit Calvin with it. It was huge. About the size of a cow's lower leg. Meat Of The Matter Butcher Shop sells bones like that. They don't let anything go to waste. I wonder if it came from there. I'm sure Hank has checked it out. Maybe the robber didn't even mean to kill Calvin. He wanted to escape the shelter and fast. Druggies can act desperately."

The tune on the restaurant's sound system changed, and "Whole Lotta Shakin' Goin' On" filled the room. I tapped my foot to the beat of one of my favorite tunes. If I were at home right now, Porkchop and I would be dancing around my living room.

"You are assuming it is a man. What if a woman killed Calvin?" Candie wiped away a dollop of mayonnaise clinging to her pinkie finger.

I nodded. "You are right, I guess I am. A woman could have murdered him as well." My phone jangled in my purse. Reading the caller ID, I recognized the animal hospital's number on the caller ID. "What could they want?" I said and flipped open my phone.

"Um, yeah, sure. I can come at closing. Thanks. I appreciate Doc finding the book for me." I heaved a big sigh and snapped my phone shut.

"What was your call all about?" Candie asked. She slipped her napkin back onto her lap.

"Guess I got caught in my own lie. It was Jeanine. She believed my story—when I dropped Porkchop off for his mani-pedi—about writing an article on Japanese Spitz. But then again, why wouldn't she? She knows I am a writer since I interviewed Doc about his career as a vet. He has a book about Hana's breed and is willing to lend it to me."

A puzzled look shrouded Candie's face.

"You know, when I tried to pry information out of her about Patsy Ikeda and Hana."

Candie nodded. "Oh, yeah. Suspect number one."

"I can't exactly tell her I don't want the book now. She said to stop by the animal hospital after closing, around sixish."

I swallowed the last bite of romaine lettuce I could coax my stomach to endure, then reached for my purse. I had errands to run before meeting with Jeanine at six. I slid out of the booth and grabbed my check. I promised Candie I'd call her after meeting with Jeanine.

* * *

"Porkchop, with all this investigation into Calvin's murder, I've neglected you. How about if you come with me tonight when I grab the book Jeanine has for me?"

Porkchop lay snuggled next to my hip on the sofa. He eyed the biscotti I had dunked into my tea.

I know, I know. After my salad, my resolve to eat better had gone down the tubes. But these cookies contained fewer calories than say a slice of apple pie. Boy, was I ever good at rationalizing?

With the last dip of the biscotti into my tea, my eyelids started to droop. I placed my mug on a flea market find side table I had painted white, trying to give it a shabby chic style. "Are you tired, too, Porkchop?" His eyelids closed to half-mast. "We'll take a little snooze before heading over to the vet's." I drew an afghan Memaw Parker had crocheted around Porkchop and myself. A couple of minutes of rest and I'd be fine. They were my "power naps." After about twenty minutes of snooze time, I could tackle the world.

"Eeewwww. Stop! Stop!" Who would have thought Daniel Craig was such a sloppy kisser? I mean he plays James Bond, after all. I reached out to shove him away and got a fist full of fur. My eyelids flew open. Porkchop was slobbering on my cheek. No wet kisses from Mr. Bond. "Okay, I'm awake. Are you hungry?" Porkchop jumped off the sofa and yelped what I interpreted to mean "You bet I am, and I want my kibbles, now!"

I gazed at the clock on my cable box as I strolled into the kitchen. Five thirty. "Yikes, Porkchop, we have got to get a move on, or we'll be late for our meeting with Jeanine." I dumped kibbles into his bowl then hurried to make myself presentable with a quick comb through the hair and a swipe of lipstick.

* * *

"Be good and maybe Jeanine will have a treat for you." Porkchop wagged his tail as I snapped on his leash. We had made it to the animal hospital with five minutes to spare.

Jeanine walked out from behind the receptionist's desk when we entered the hospital. I sneezed. The smell of Jacob's doggie perfume permeated the air.

"It has a strong scent." I waved my hand in front of my nose and tried to dispel the worst of it. I wanted to keep from having a sneezing fit.

Jeanine grimaced. "Tell me about it! Clients can't resist spritzing it on themselves and their pets. It clings to all my clothes. I can't get away from it."

My eyes traveled around the waiting room. An eerie empty atmosphere hung over the usually bustling room. "This place looks unusually quiet. I've never come here without a few patients in the waiting room."

"It's only me here right now. Our night-time tech assistant is running late, something about his babysitter getting sick and having to find another. I volunteered to stay until he finds someone."

"How nice of you. We never had such a problem, did we?" I said.

"No, we didn't go forth and multiply," Jeanine replied.

Something about her answer niggled at my brain. Where had I heard that before?

Jeanine reached down and petted Porkchop. "I will fetch the book for you. Porkchop, Doc has some special treats in his office. Want one?" She stared up at me. "Okay with you?"

I unclipped Porkchop's leash. "Sure, you said the magic word."

Jeanine gave me a puzzled look.

I laughed. "Treat. Say the word and he will follow you anywhere."

Porkchop waddled after Jeanine. Little did I know he was following her into danger.

CHAPTER TWENTY-FOUR

———

I glanced at my watch. Worry slithered up my spine. What was keeping Jeanine and Porkchop? Five minutes had passed since my baby trotted after Jeanine in search of the book Doc had left for me. I rose from the wooden bench and rubbed my rear to get the circulation going again. These park-style benches may be animal friendly, but they weren't people's-rear-end friendly.

I approached the reception counter and leaned over and called out. "Jeanine, everything all right?"

"Yes, yes. I'm having a little trouble finding the book Doc left. His desk is piled high with paperwork."

"If you can't find the book, it's okay. I can do research online," I shouted. "I don't want Porkchop causing trouble."

A high pitch giggle answered me back. "He's fine, enjoying the special treats Doc keeps on his desk for his favorite clients. Porkchop surely is a favorite. I'm sure the book will turn up in a minute."

I walked back to the bench and sat. It might be steaming hot outside, but something about Jeanine's high-pitched laugh shot a chill through my body. I rubbed my arms to ward off the goose bumps riding piggyback. My crossed legs pumped up and down like an oil rig gone crazy. I glanced at my wrist and saw that another five minutes had dragged by. Enough, already.

I rose and strode to a swinging metal door. It separated the reception area from the hospital's nether region. I gingerly pushed open the door and peeked around it. I'd only been in the exam room area of the hospital. A myriad of other rooms ran along the back of the building—offices, lab rooms, storage areas, also the boarding area. For some reason, I sensed the need to tiptoe down the hall. I didn't want to alert Jeanine I was looking for her. Something was off with her. I couldn't put my finger on it, but her maniacal laugh sent red caution flags up in my mind.

I peeked into the various rooms. The room that served as Doc's office was anyone's guess. I cocked my head and heard singing. The song led me to the back of the hospital. As I walked closer to the source of the music, I noticed it was a lullaby. Maybe they played them to soothe the pets boarding here. I crept closer to the tune. It came from a room at the end of the hall. The sight in front of me when I peered into the room shocked me.

From all the cardboard boxes lining the walls, it must be a storage room. The boxes all sported various labels from paper towels to syringes. Bags of pet food were stacked next to the door. Jeanine sat cross-legged on the floor in the middle of the room. Her mouth twisted into a malevolent grin reminiscent of the Joker in the *Batman* movies. While she hadn't painted her face white, an exaggerated red mouth spread across her face. Mascara ran down her cheeks from the streaming tears. Gone was the mousy Jeanine replaced by a deranged version of herself. Her hair was loosened from its usual neat braid and hung wildly about her shoulders. Unaware of my presence, she rocked back and forth singing "Rock-a-bye-Baby" with my Porkchop cradled in her arms.

My knees shook. I clutched the door jamb to keep from sinking to the floor. "Porkchop." I choked on the fear clogging my throat. What had she done to my Porkchop? He lay swaddled in a blanket in her arms, eyes shut and head lolling to the side. "Porkchop," I called out again. I stepped into the room. My dog didn't respond. Tears sprang to my eyes. Why wouldn't he look at me?

Finally, Jeanine noticed I had entered the room. She blinked her eyes rapidly and tried to focus on me. "You know, I didn't want to kill him."

I gasped. My heart pounded in my chest. "What did you do to my Porkchop?" I lunged towards her.

"Not Porkchop, silly, Calvin Perkins. He threatened to tell Momma why I couldn't have children. You know 'go forth and multiply' as Momma always preached. He wanted more money from me, but I couldn't afford it. Keeping Momma in Shady Oaks has become expensive. They increased their fees. Calvin was evil, you know. And Momma says the Lord wants us to banish evil from the earth. I got pregnant with Jacob's baby, but he didn't want our baby. He said we were too young. We'd have plenty of time to make babies in the future. He took me to a butcher Calvin had recommended. Things went wrong and I can never 'go forth and multiply.' So, I only did the Lord's work." Her stringy hair dangled in her face. She looked at Porkchop and clutched his limp body to her chest and rocked back and forth humming the lullaby.

I took another step towards her. As I gazed at Porkchop, I thought my heart would burst with hope. I prayed harder than I ever had in my life that he would be all right. His chest still moved up and down, but from the way his head rested on her arm with his eyes closed, he acted like he was drugged. I reached out one of my hands towards Jeanine and pleaded, "I understand. We all do foolish things when we're young. I don't blame you for being upset with Calvin. He's hurt a great deal of people." My voice clogged with tears. "But please—Porkchop, he didn't have anything to do with this."

"I know, but you are poking your nose into Calvin's murder. Asking all those questions. You have to stop, or Momma will find out." She slid her hand under her skirt and pulled out a loaded syringe. "Promise me no more questions or I may have to take your baby away from you. Like I lost my baby."

Her hand started to descend towards Porkchop. The sharp needle aimed at his neck.

"Please, nooo." My scream ripped out of my throat.

A voice boomed behind me. "Miss Wagner, this is the police. Drop the needle, now."

Jeanine's glazed eyes darted to the person standing behind me. Hank. He nudged his way next to me. She looked from Hank to Porkchop. His presence distracted her from her evil purpose long enough for me to race towards her and kick the syringe out of her hand. I grabbed my precious pup from her lap then ripped the blanket from his body and clutched him to me. He stirred in my arms. Whatever she had given him must not have been that strong since he opened one of his beautiful brown eyes at me and nuzzled my hand.

Hank pulled Jeanine from the floor. As he read her rights, he firmly clamped handcuffs around her wrists. Then he called the police station for assistance.

Jeanine looked at me as Hank led her out of the room. "You know, Calvin really was a bad person."

I had to agree with her. Calvin had hurt a lot of people, but it wasn't up to me to judge him or Jeanine either.

CHAPTER TWENTY-FIVE

———

Hank and I stood next to his unmarked car. "How did you know I was here?" I asked, looking into his crystal blue eyes.

"I was driving by and noticed your Bug in the parking lot. Since it was after hospital office hours, I got worried something was wrong with my buddy here." Hank scratched Porkchop's head, who responded by licking his hand.

My dog was acting fully recovered now from the so-called treat Jeanine had fed him to make him more docile. When the other officers had arrived at the animal hospital, she confessed to dipping it in a sleeping aid. From working at the vet's for over thirty years she was well acquainted with some of the meds used on the dogs and how to administer them. While Jeanine was being taken into custody, I made a quick call to Doc Sorenson. Within minutes he arrived at the hospital and checked Porkchop over. My fears were relieved when he said Porkchop would make a full recovery.

I nodded towards the police car where Jeanine sat in the back seat, mumbling to herself. "Poor Jeanine. What will become of her now? She looks to have had some sort of breakdown. What could have pushed her over the edge? Was it her overbearing mother or Calvin's blackmail?"

Hank shook his head. "We'll leave it for the courts to determine, but a good lawyer might be able to prove she's mentally unbalanced. The judge might go lighter on her."

Hank pointed to my car. "Are you all right to drive home?"

I nodded. "I will be fine. Especially now since Doc said Porkchop will be okay." Hank scratched Porkchop behind the ears then climbed into his car. He rolled down his window.

"Since this case is solved, I'll give you a call. If it is all right with you?"

My jaw dropped open. "Ummm, sure," I stammered then waved as he pulled out of the parking lot.

* * *

"Sam." Gladys squealed and tugged me into her house. A few friends had gathered to celebrate Frank being cleared of Calvin's murder.

"How's this cute little poochie pooh?" Gladys cooed over Porkchop. After learning of his ordeal at the hospital, she'd insisted he attend the party, too.

"He's fine, completely recovered. Doc checked him over." Extra treats had helped the process.

"Hey, cousin," Candie said, as she and Mark made their way across the living room. Candie enveloped me in a hug. "My knees still go weak when I think of the danger you were in," she whispered into my ear.

I pulled back and saw a tear trembling on her eyelash. "I do too, cuz. Believe me, it's one experience I don't want to repeat. I never suspected Jeanine. She seemed so meek and mild. Maybe Frank with his drug-selling past, Jacob having a gambling problem, and Patsy afraid of losing her beloved Hana. They all seemed to have viable reasons to kill Calvin when we first suspected them. They had something in their past they wanted to hide. But Jeanine?" I shook my head in disbelief.

Candie nodded. "She was terrified of her mother. Calvin threatening to tell her mother if Jeanine didn't come up with more money just pushed her over the edge. She was an easy victim for Calvin, and he knew how to play her."

"She confessed to Hank that she put the dog poop and note in my car hoping I'd stop my snooping. Guess she didn't know how stubborn we Parkers can be. Hers was the car I heard squealing out of the parking lot, too. I feel so sorry for her and hope she gets the help she needs."

Candie's face paled. "You almost walked in on her whacking Calvin with the bone."

"Yes, but thank heavens I didn't. Hefting those forty-pound bags of dog food around the vet's must have given her that 'strong arm' we talked about. I squeezed her arm, then noticed Mark standing behind her holding two cold microbrews.

"Where can a gal get one of those?" I asked, smiling.

Gladys responded to my request and shouted, "Hey, Junior! Bring the lady of the hour a beer!"

I chuckled then turned towards the kitchen door. Striding out of the kitchen towards me came Detective Hank Johnson or as Candie would say, "Hunky" Hank. And in those tight-fitting jeans, he without a doubt, fit the nickname.

"Junior?" I asked, raising an eyebrow.

"What can I say? Dad's Hank Senior, so the family has always called me Junior." He handed me the beer and saluted me with his. "Here's to getting to know you...off duty."

I smiled and tipped back my beer. I only hoped it cooled off the heat rising in my cheeks.

ABOUT THE AUTHOR

Syrl Ann Kazlo, a retired teacher, lives in upstate New York with her husband and two very lively dachshunds. Kibbles and Death is the first book in her Samantha Davies Mystery series, featuring Samantha Davies and her lovable dachshund, Porkchop. When not writing Syrl is busy hooking—rug hooking that is—reading, and enjoying her family. She is a member of Sisters in Crime and the Mavens of Mayhem.

Learn more about S.A. Kazlo at:
www.sakazlo.com

Made in the USA
Monee, IL
11 November 2022

17532119R00100